'A masterpiece . . . a mesmeric study of individual and collective guilt' *Daily Mail*

'If you like Simenon and Japrisot you'll love Philippe Claudel' *Elle*

'A sumptuous novel whose theme bears comparison with the great Russians' *Le Monde*

'Unforgettable' *France Soir*

'A beautiful novel, we don't read them like this nowadays, they don't write them like this, what a writer!'
Le Nouvel Observateur

'Overwhelming . . . the language is magnificent, each word resonates, each sentence paints a picture' *Le Parisien*

D1321786

Philippe Claudel was born in 1962. He has won several awards in France for his fiction, including the Prix Goncourt for the Short Story in 2003.

Grey Souls

PHILIPPE CLAUDEL

Translated by Adriana Hunter

PHOENIX

A PHOENIX PAPERBACK

First published in Great Britain in 2005
by Phoenix House
This paperback edition published in 2006
by Phoenix,
an imprint of Orion Books Ltd,
Orion House, 5 Upper St Martin's Lane
London WC2H 9EA

First published in French as *Les Âmes Grises*
by Editions Stock, Paris

1 3 5 7 9 10 8 6 4 2

Copyright © Philippe Claudel 2005
Translation copyright © Adriana Hunter 2005

The right of Philippe Claudel to be identified as the author
of this work has been asserted by him in accordance with
the Copyright, Designs and Patents Act 1988.

The right of Adriana Hunter to be identified as the translator
of this work has been asserted by her in accordance with the
Copyright, Designs and Patents Act 1988.

This book is supported by the French Ministry for Foreign Affairs,
as part of the Burgess programme headed for the French Embassy in
London by the Institut Français du Royaume-Uni.

Liberté • Égalité • Fraternité
RÉPUBLIQUE FRANÇAISE

A CIP catalogue record for this book is
available from the British Library.

ISBN-13 978-0-7538-2061-2
ISBN-10 0-7538-2061-7

Printed and bound in Great Britain by
Clays Ltd, St Ives plc

The Orion Publishing Group's policy is to use papers that are natural,
renewable and recyclable products and made from wood grown in sustainable
forests. The logging and manufacturing processes are expected to conform
to the environmental regulations of the country of origin.

www.orionbooks.co.uk

Je suis là. Mon destin est d'être là.

Jean-Claude Pirotte, *Un voyage en automne*

Être le greffier du temps
quelconque assesseur que l'on voit rôder
lorsque se mélangent l'homme et la lumière.

Jean-Claude Tardif, *L'Homme de peu*

In memory of André Vers

i

I don't quite know where to begin. It's not easy. So much time has passed and the words are gone for ever. The faces too, the smiles, the wounds. Even so, I must try to explain what has been eating at my heart these past twenty years. The remorse, the questions that have weighed me down. I must take a knife to the belly of this mystery and plunge my hands inside, although nothing can change what happened.

If they ask me by what miracle I know the things I am about to reveal, I will say that I *know*, that's all. These things are as familiar to me as nightfall and sunrise. I have spent my life trying to piece them together, to make them speak so I can listen. That was my job in a way once upon a time.

I will parade before you a whole host of shadows, but one of them in particular will stand out. This is the ghost of a man called Pierre-Ange Destinat, the Public Prosecutor in the town of V for more than thirty years. He pursued his profession with clockwork precision, prone neither to emotion nor mechanical failure. A true work of art, you might say, and he needed no museum to be seen at his best. In 1917, at the time of the *Affaire* (as the locals called it, underscoring the capital letter with sighs and grimaces), Destinat was over sixty years old and had been retired for a year. A tall, lean man, he looked like an eagle, or some other majestic bird, cold and aloof. He said little, but when he spoke his words carried great weight. He had pale eyes that never seemed to flicker. His thin upper lip was clean-shaven, his forehead high, his hair grey.

V is about twenty kilometres from our town. In 1917, it might as well have been a world away, especially in winter, and with the war going on and on. The fighting brought chaos to our narrow roads, lorries and carts filled them, and then there was the stench of smoke. The front was quite close, so we heard the thunder of the explosions, but far enough away to seem like an invisible monster lurking on the other side of the hill, a country hidden from our view.

Destinat was called many things, depending on where he was and who was talking about him. Most of the inmates of the prison in V called him the Blood-letter. In one of the cells I even saw a picture of him, carved with a knife into a heavy oak door. It was actually quite a good likeness. Mind you, during his two-week trial, the artist had had plenty of time to observe the sitter.

If any of us met Pierre-Ange Destinat in the street, we called him by his title: Monsieur le Procureur. The men would raise their caps and the humbler women would curtsey. Grander ladies, from his own world, would simply lower their heads, like little birds sipping from a gutter. He made no reply. Or he did, but you would have needed four well-polished lorgnettes to see his lips move. I don't think his reaction was contempt (though others did); it was more like detachment.

There was one person who almost understood him, a young woman, about whom I shall go into more detail later. She and she alone had a nickname of her own for him: Sorrow. It could have been her fault that it all happened – even though she never knew anything about it.

At the beginning of the century, a public prosecutor was still an important person. And in wartime, when a splattering of machine-gun fire could flatten a whole company of strapping young men, it required a certain skill to ask for the death of one solitary, shackled man. In my opinion, it was not for cruelty's sake that he asked for – and was usually granted – the head of some poor bugger who'd battered a postman to death or disembowelled his mother-in-law. The accused would stand before him, an idiot handcuffed between two policemen, but Destinat hardly saw him. He would look right through the man as if he were already gone. He wasn't attacking a flesh-and-blood criminal, but defending an idea. An idea, that was it. His own idea of good and evil.

The condemned man would howl as sentence was passed, weeping, raging, his hands raised to heaven as if suddenly remembering his catechism. But the man was already gone, as far as Destinat was concerned. He would gather up his notes, four or five sheets of paper on which he had inscribed his summing-up in his tiny, refined hand. A few well-chosen words in violet ink, words which made the courtroom shudder, and gave the jury food for thought (if they were still awake). Words that could build a scaffold in no time, more quickly and more surely than two journeymen carpenters.

Destinat did not hold a grudge against this condemned man who was no longer there. I once saw this with my own eyes at the end of a trial: Destinat came out into the corridor like Cato the elder, still in his magnificent ermine, and there was the man about to be wedded to the guillotine. He called out plaintively, eyes still red from the shock of the sentence, regretting now, of course, the shots he had fired into his boss's stomach: 'M'sieur l'Procureur. M'sieur l'Procureur . . .' and Destinat looked right at him, oblivious to the policemen and the handcuffs, and he put a hand on the man's shoulder as he replied: 'My friend. We've met somewhere before, I think? What can I do for you?' There was no mockery in his tone. He spoke sincerely. But for the other man it was as if a second sentence had been passed on him.

After the trial, Destinat would lunch at Le Rébillon across the road from the cathedral. The *patron* was a big man with a yellow-and-white head like a heart of chicory, and a big mouthful of rotten teeth. His name was Bourrache. He was not a very clever man but he was canny with money. It was second nature to him, not something he could be criticised for. He always wore a large blue apron, which made him look like a belted barrel. At one time there had been a wife who took to her bed and languished (as we used to say). You often see this kind of thing with women who confuse the November fog with their own unhappiness. But then she died, not so much as a result of her illness, which she must have become quite attached to, but because of what happened. The *Affaire*.

In those days the Bourraches' three daughters were like lilies, with a hint of pure red blood which made the colour in their cheeks burn. The youngest was not yet ten. She was unlucky. Or was she very lucky? I don't know.

The other two were known only by their first names: Aline and Rose. But the little one was known to all as Belle. The fancier types sometimes dressed it up as Belle de jour after the flower. When they were all there together, taking round cutlery, jugs of water and carafes of wine, they made me think of three budding flowers dropped in a seedy tavern. To me, the youngest one always seemed so fresh that you would have thought she belonged to another world altogether.

When Destinat walked into the restaurant, Bourrache, never very original, always served up the same corny line. 'One less to worry about then, eh, Monsieur le Procureur?' Destinat never bothered to reply. Bourrache would show him to his table – oh, yes, Destinat had his own table, permanently reserved, one of the best. Not *the* best – because there was one, nestling by the big wood stove and with commanding views of the Place du Palais through the lace curtains – that was reserved for Judge Mierck. Judge Mierck was a regular. He came four times a week, as his bulging belly and blotchy skin testified. His face looked as if every glass of Burgundy he had drunk had taken up residence there. Mierck did not like the Prosecutor and the feeling was mutual, no exaggeration. But you would often see them say hello, doffing hats, like men with nothing to unite them who, all the same, have to share the same daily life.

The strange thing was that Destinat did not go to Le Rébillon very often, and yet there was his table, empty for most of the year, representing quite a loss of income for Bourrache. Nothing, but nothing, would have made him give it to anyone else, though, even when the big country show was on, when every last peasant in the region was there wanting to gorge himself in between a morning prodding cows' backsides (having already downed a good litre of plum brandy since dawn) and a night in Ma Nain's brothel. The table sat empty as people were turned away. Bourrache even threw someone out for insisting on it, a livestock merchant who never came back.

'Better the King's table and no King, than some old customer with cow muck on his shoes!' That's what Bourrache told me one day when I was going on at him about it.

ii

It was the first Monday of December 1917 and the weather was bitterly cold. Like Siberia. The ground rang beneath my heels, and the noise reverberated up my body to my neck. I remember the big blanket that had been thrown over the child's body, how quickly it was soaked through. And the two policemen, Berfuche (a dumpy little man with hairy ears like a wild pig) and Grosspeil (whose family had emigrated from Alsace forty years earlier). They stood guard over her, close to the river bank. Hanging back a little was the Bréchut boy, a tubby lad with hair like a brush, fiddling with the ends of his knitted waistcoat, not knowing quite what to do, to stay or to leave. He had found her in the water, on his way to the harbour-master's office where he worked as a clerk. He works there still, only now he is twenty years older, and his scalp is as shiny as an ice floe.

It's not very big, a ten-year-old's body, particularly one that's soaked in wintry water. Berfuche lifted a corner of the blanket, then blew on his hands to warm them. Belle de jour's face appeared. Crows flew silently overhead.

She was a fairy-tale princess with blue lips and white eyelids. Her hair mingled with the frost-rusted grass, and her little hands closed tightly around emptiness. As we puffed like bulls, warm breath on cold air, our moustaches became covered with ice. We stamped to bring some feeling back to our feet. Geese circled the sky clumsily, as if they had lost their way. The sun was huddled in a fraying coat of fog. Even the distant guns seemed to be frozen. There was no sound.

'Peace at last maybe,' Grosspeil ventured.

'Peace, my arse!' his colleague retorted, pulling the sodden blanket back over the child's body.

The men from V arrived at last. The mayor was with them, wearing his not-a-good-day face; the one you put on when you're hauled out of bed at some ungodly hour in weather you wouldn't put a dog out in. Judge Mierck was there too, and his clerk, whose name I never knew but who was always called Crusty because of a patch of eczema that disfigured the left-hand side of his face. With them were three self-important police officers, and a soldier. I don't know what the soldier was doing there, and he didn't stay long, passing out almost straight away and having to be carried off to Jacques's café. The strutting cock can't ever have been close to a bayonet except in an armoury, if then! You could tell from his impeccably pressed and tailored uniform. He looked like a shop mannequin. His war was being fought from a big velvet arm-chair next to a nice cast-iron stove, and rehashed for young ladies in ball gowns at evening parties, crystal chandeliers overhead, champagne flute in hand, the bewigged oom-pah-pah of a chamber orchestra playing in the background.

Beneath his Cronstadt hat and replete exterior, Judge Mierck was an abrupt man. All those rich sauces might have reddened his ears and nose, but they had not softened him. He pulled back the blanket himself and looked at Belle de jour for a long time. We waited for a word, a sigh. After all, he knew her well, saw her almost every day when he went to gorge himself at Le Rébillon. But he looked at the little body as if it

[7]

were a stone or a piece of wood. Without heart. His eye as icy as the water flowing nearby.

'It's Bourrache's youngest,' someone whispered, as if to say: 'Poor little thing. Only ten. And she was bringing you bread and smoothing your tablecloth yesterday.' He snapped round towards whoever had dared to speak. 'What bloody difference does that make to me? A dead body is a dead body!'

Before all this, we'd always thought of him just as Judge Mierck, end of story. He had his place in life and he fitted it, not much liked but respected. But after what he said on that first Monday in December, in front of that child's soaking corpse . . . and there was the way he said it, so curtly, almost happily, his eyes lighting up at the thought of a murder, a real murder at last (and it was murder, that was obvious) and in wartime when every assassin went jobless in civilian life the better to toil in uniform. After that response, the whole region turned its back on him, and no one could think of him without disgust.

'Good, good, good, good . . .' he hummed as if he were heading off to play skittles or go shooting. Then, just like that, he was hungry, had to have soft-boiled eggs, 'soft-boiled, not hard!' straight away. Had to have them right there, beside the little canal, in minus ten degrees, next to Belle de jour's body. That shocked us too.

One of the three policemen, the one who had just got back from dropping off the wilting officer, dashed straight off again to find some eggs for Mierck. 'Not just eggs, little worlds, little worlds,' was what the Judge used to say as he cracked open the shells with a miniature silver hammer kept specially on his fob for such an occasion, because he quite often made this capricious request for eggs, savouring them greedily so that the yolk clung to his moustache.

While he waited for his eggs, he surveyed the scene, whistling quietly to himself, hands lightly clasped behind his back. We were just trying to keep ourselves warm. And on he talked, there was no stopping him. I had heard him call her Belle de jour before but now she was 'the victim', as if death could take away not only life but the pretty names of flowers.

'You fished the victim out, did you?'

The Bréchut boy is still fumbling with his waistcoat as if he wants to hide in it. He nods, and Mierck asks whether the cat's got his tongue. The boy shakes his head. This irritates the judge who's beginning to lose the good mood the murder put him in, particularly as the policeman is still not back with the eggs. Then the Bréchut boy manages a few details and the judge listens, going 'good, good, good . . .' under his breath from time to time.

The minutes pass. It is still just as cold. The geese fly off. The water flows on. One corner of the blanket dips in and the current catches it, folds it, like a hand beating a rhythm, down and up. But the judge sees none of this. He is listening to the boy's statement, missing nothing, eggs forgotten. The youth's account was still clear at this stage, but by the time he had tramped it round all the cafés the story had become an epic and he was being stood drinks by everybody. By midnight he was blind drunk, bawling out the child's name in a shaking voice, pissing his pants after all the wine they had bought for him. At the end of the night, filthy and pickled as a herring, he could only mime it, beautifully, serious and dramatic, his gestures rendered all the more eloquent by the wine.

Judge Mierck's great backside spilled over the seat of his shooting stick, a tripod of camel skin and ebony which had really impressed us all the first few times he produced it. Ah the colonies . . . he had spent three years chasing chicken-thieves and grain-looters around Ethiopia, or something like that. He used to open it out and put it away over and over again at crime scenes, sitting on it like a painter gazing at his model. You knew when he was itching for a fight; he'd throw that stick in the air and twirl it around like a round-handled baton.

The judge listened and ate (the eggs had arrived at last, in a steaming white cloth, carried by a breathless police officer who now stood solemnly to attention). The judge's moustache was yellow and grey. He ground the shells beneath the heel of his boot as he wiped his lips with a large lawn handkerchief. The noise was like delicate bird bones shattering. Fragments clung to his boots like tiny spurs while nearby, just a few paces away, the child lay beneath her shroud of sodden wool. She had not spoiled the judge's eggs. In fact I think her presence made them all the tastier.

Bréchut finished his account as the judge, ever the connoisseur, munched through his 'little worlds'. 'Good, good, good . . .' he said, standing up and brushing down his shirt front, eyes diving into the countryside around us, still absolutely straight with his hat sitting just so.

Morning trickled out its sequence of hours. We were rooted there like toy figures in a miniature landscape. Berfuche's nose had gone red and his eyes were streaming. Grosspeil was turning the colour of the water. Crusty held his notebook in which he had already made some notes, and occasionally scratched his sore cheek, now mottled white with cold. The policeman who had brought the eggs looked as if he were made of wax. The mayor had gone back gratefully to his warm office, his small duty complete. What happened now was of no concern to him.

The judge sucked down great lungfuls of blue air, hopping from foot to foot, hands behind his back. We were waiting for Victor Desharet, the doctor from V. But the judge was in no hurry now. He was savouring the moment, inscribing it in his memory, with all the other crime scenes and murderous landscapes. His own private museum. I am sure that trawling through it gave him no less of a thrill than the murderers themselves experienced. The line between hunter and hunted is very fine.

The doctor turns up: he and the judge make quite a pair. They were at school together, and they have that way of talking, call each other 'tu', but it sounds odd in their mouths, as if they're really saying 'vous'. They often lunch together, at Le Rébillon and other restaurants. These meals go on for hours, and they'll eat anything, but they particularly like charcuterie and offal: brawn, tripe with cream, breaded pig's trotters, brains, fried kidneys. They have known each other for such a long time that they have begun to resemble each other: same colouring, same fat neck, same belly, same detached eyes that register neither the filth in the streets nor any sign of compassion.

The doctor, Desharet, looks at the body as if it were something in one of his textbooks. Obviously he doesn't want to get his gloves wet, but I know that he too knew the child well. In his hands, though, she is no longer a child, just a corpse. He touches the lips, lifts the eyelids, loosens the clothes at her neck, and that is when we see them, the purple blotches circling her throat like a necklace. 'Strangulation!' he pronounces. No need to have been to a fancy university to work that out, but even so, there on that icy morning, so close to the little body, the word hits us like a slap in the face.

'Good, good, good . . .' went the judge again, with relish, eager to sink his teeth into this one; a real murder, and a child, too, and – could it be better? – a little girl. He turned on his heel, smug and simpering, moustache all eggy, and said: 'Oh, what's this door then?'

We all looked at the door, as if it had just appeared like the Virgin Mary, a little door breaching a long, high wall, behind which we could see a park, a real serious park with serious trees; and behind the trees with their naked, interwoven branches, a house, a grand rambling mansion, the residence of an important man.

'Well, it leads into the grounds of the château . . .' It was Bréchut who answered.

'Oh, a château . . .' the judge mocked.

'Well, yes, the Prosecutor's château.'

'Fancy that. So this is where it is . . .' said the judge, more to himself than to us, who meant less than shrew droppings to him by then anyway. You would have thought he was delighted to hear the man's name mentioned, and in connection with such a horrible murder: his rival, the man he hated, nobody knew why, unless it was because hating was what he did, Judge Mierck, and all he could do, his nature.

'Good, good, good . . .' he began again, cheerful all of a sudden, slamming his great behind down on the exotic seat, positioning himself right across from the little door which opened onto the grounds of the château. And he stayed like that for an eternity, freezing steadily like a bullfinch on a washing line, while we stamped out feet and blew on our gloved hands, and young Bréchut lost the feeling in his nose and Crusty turned a purplish grey.

It has to be said that the château, so imposing with its brick walls and slated roofs, was really something, a kind of jewel in the wealthy *quartier* of our town, and yes, we did have one. We had a hospital too, constantly full in those years of universal slaughter; and two schools, one for girls, one for boys; and a factory, a huge one, with chimneys reaching up to the sky and spewing out plumes of sooty smoke day and night, summer and winter. Since it was built in the late 1880s, the factory had kept the whole region going, and there were very few men in the town who did not work there. They had abandoned the fields and the vineyards for it, and now the weeds and brambles ran riot over the hillside, gobbling up the orchards, the vines and the furrows of good soil.

Our town was not very large. It was not V, far from it. Still, you could get lost in it, by which I mean that it had shadowy nooks and isolated spots enough for anybody who wanted to nurse their melancholy. To the factory we owed the hospital, the schools and the carefully stocked little library.

The owner of the factory had no name or face. It was a 'group', as they say, a 'consortium' if you really want to sound smart. Rows of houses had sprung up where there were once cereal crops, little streets all exactly the same. Houses rented out in exchange for very little (just silence, obedience, and no industrial disputes) to workers who had never dreamed of such luxury, and who felt strange peeing into a lavatory rather than a hole in a pine plank. The old farms, the few that held out against progress, huddled round the church as if by instinct, cherishing their old walls and low windows, exhaling the sour smell of cow dung and curdled milk through half-open barn doors.

The factory even dug two canals for us, a big one for the barges that delivered coal and limestone, and took away sodium ash, and a smaller one to keep the water level in the big one topped up. They took a good ten years to build. Gentlemen in ties, pockets stuffed with banknotes, wandered about the place at that time, buying up land left, right and centre. There was so much free drink you could stay drunk from one end of the month to the next. Then one day they were gone and our town belonged to them. After that, everyone sobered up. After that, people had to work. For them.

Back to the château – it would not be untrue to say that it was the most imposing residence in the town. Old Destinat, I mean our man's father, had it built just after the disaster at Sedan. And he certainly did not skimp. People in these parts may not say much, but they make their mark by other means. The Prosecutor spent his whole life there. In fact, he went one better than that, for he was born there and he died there.

The château was huge, not on a human scale at all, particularly as they were never a numerous family. Once old Destinat's son was born, he hung up his boots, officially satisfied. Which didn't stop him impregnating a few bellies with very pretty bastards, to each of whom he gave a gold coin every year until they were twenty-one when they received a handsome letter of recommendation, along with a symbolic kick up the backside to ensure that they went and checked – somewhere very far away – that the world was indeed round.

In these parts, they call that generosity. Not everyone would do as much.

The Prosecutor was the last of the Destinats. There will be no more. He did marry, but his wife died six months after the wedding, to which incidentally every person of fortune and note in the whole region came. She had been a de Vincey before her marriage and her ancestors had fought at Crécy. Ours probably had too, but no one knows for sure and no one cares.

In the hallway of the Château hung a portrait of her from the time of her marriage, painted by a man who came all the way from Paris. The thing that struck you about it was how he had managed to capture in her face some hint of her imminent demise, the deathly pallor of her skin, the resignation in her features. She was called Clélia. An unusual name, prettily carved in the pink marble of her tomb.

An entire regiment could have been billeted with space to spare in the grounds of the château. The park was surrounded by water and at the far end there was a little communal path which served as a short cut between the *mairie* and the loading dock, then there was the little canal I have already mentioned, over which the old man had had a Japanese bridge built. People called it the *Boudin* because it was painted the colour of those white blood sausages. On the far bank you could see the big windows of a tall building. This was the factory laboratory where engineers devised ways of making more money for their masters. To the right of the park, a narrow river wound sinuously through eddies and water lilies, its name, the Guerlante, perfectly suggesting both garland and sloth. Water seeped into everything. The château grounds resembled an expanse of sodden cloth, and the grass dripped incessantly. It was a perfect place to catch a chill.

Which is exactly what happened to Clélia Destinat. It was

all over and done with in the space of three weeks, between the doctor's first visit and the gravedigger's last slow shovelful of dirt. 'Why do you pour that shovelful so slowly?' I once asked Ostrane the gravedigger. 'Because that one,' he replied, looking at me with his dark, bottomless eyes, 'that particular one should stick in the memory . . .' Ostrane can talk and he likes to stir things up. He missed his calling; he should have gone on the stage.

Old Destinat had come straight from the land, but in fifty years he had managed somehow to clean himself up, towelling himself off with banknotes and sacks of gold. He moved into a different world, employed six hundred people, owned five tenanted farms, eight hundred hectares of woodland (entirely oak), pasture as far as the eye could see, ten apartment blocks in V, and a good cushion of decent shares – none of your Panamas for him – big enough for ten men to rest their heads on without their elbows getting in the way.

He received and was received everywhere. At the bishop's palace or the police commissioner's house. He was now someone.

I have not mentioned old Madame Destinat. She was quite another story. From the very best stock, from the land too, but from those who had always owned it rather than those who worked it. As a dowry she brought her husband more than half of what he owned, and some social polish. Then she withdrew to her books and her good works. It was her right to name their son, though, and she called him Ange, her angel. The old man added Pierre. He felt that Ange lacked spirit and virility. She never saw her boy after that, or hardly. Between the English nannies and the Jesuit boarding school, time passed more quickly than the batting of an eyelid. She gave away a whimpering child with pink cheeks and puffy eyes, and one day she got back a rather stiff young fellow with three hairs and two pimples on his chin. He looked down at her like a real little gentleman, crammed with Latin and Greek, and with his own importance and his dreams of romantic conquest.

She died as she lived, withdrawn from the world. Few even realised. The son was in Paris studying law and came back for the funeral, even more buffed up by the big city and its sparkling conversation, with his light wooden cane, his impeccable collar, his upper lip now boasting a thin moustache waxed *à la Jaubert*, the last word in style! The old man ordered the most beautiful coffin. It was the only time in his life that the cabinetmaker got to work with rosewood and mahogany. The handles were gold, real gold. A vault was built with a bronze statue holding up her hands to the heavens while another knelt in silent tears: it did not mean very much, but it was beautiful to behold.

Mourning hardly changed the old man's habits at all; he simply had three suits made of black cloth, and some black crêpe armbands.

The day after the ceremony, the son went back to Paris and stayed there for many years. Then one day he reappeared, a serious man, too serious, and a public prosecutor, no longer the young fool who had tossed roses on his mother's coffin so self-importantly before dashing off to catch his train. He looked as if something had broken him inside, crushed him, but we never found out what.

Later, his own bereavement broke him for good. It distanced him too. From the world. From the rest of us. From himself, probably. I think he really loved his little hothouse flower.

Old Destinat died eight years after his wife, struck down in a ditch on his way to evict one of his tenant farmers. He was found with his mouth and nose crushed into the good, thick mud we get here in early April, thanks to the lashing rains which turn the soil to a sticky paste. He ended up right back where he started. Full circle. His money hadn't done him much good; he died like a farm boy.

Then the son was truly alone in that great house.

He went on looking down on the world, and yet it took little to please him. Once his foppish youth was gone, along with the fancy clothes and bored look, all that was left was a man who was getting on in years. His work took up all his time. In his father's day, the château had employed six gardeners, a watchman, a cook, three footmen, four chambermaids and a chauffeur. This great horde, ruled with a rod of iron, had been crammed into narrow outhouses and little rooms under the eaves where in winter the water froze in their pitchers.

The Prosecutor kept only the cook, Barbe. He thanked the others one by one and gave each of them a handsome letter and a tidy sum. Barbe took on the chambermaid's duties too and her husband – called Old Gloomy because no one, not even his wife whose own face was always creased with joy, had ever seen him smile – looked after the grounds and did odd jobs. The couple rarely went out and no one ever heard much of them, not even the Prosecutor. It was as if the house had fallen asleep. The roof of one of the turrets was leaking, a huge wisteria was smothering some of the shutters, a few cornerstones had shattered in the frost. The house was getting old, just as we all do.

Destinat never received people at the house. He had turned his back on all that. Every Sunday he went to mass, to sit in his own pew, with the family initials chiselled into the oak. He never missed a Sunday. The parish priest let his eye rest lovingly on him during the sermon, as if he were a cardinal or an accomplice. Then, when it was over, once the flock in flat caps and embroidered fichus was outside, he would walk with Destinat to the far end of the square. The bells pealed as

Destinat pulled on his kid gloves (his hands were as fine as a woman's and his fingers as slender as cigarette holders), and they would speak about something and nothing, but in the earnest tones of those who know about the human soul, by professional study or personal experience. The little display at an end, they would go back home, each to dwell on his own loneliness.

One day, one of the directors of the factory came visiting at the château. There was an exchange of cards, much bowing and scraping and lowering of hats, then he was received. This particular director was a big, cheery Belgian, with frizzy red whiskers, a bit short in the leg, dressed like someone in a novel with checked trousers and patent-leather boots. Barbe appeared with a big tray and everything they needed for tea. She served them and left. While the Director chattered away, Destinat said little, drank little, did not smoke, nor laugh, but listened politely. The other man beat about the bush, talked billiards for a good ten minutes, then partridge shooting, bridge, Havana cigars and finally the merits of French cuisine. He had been there three-quarters of an hour and was about to move on to the weather when all at once Destinat looked at his watch, quite subtly, but slowly enough for the other man to get the message.

The Director coughed, put down his cup, coughed again, picked the cup up again, then finally began: he wants to ask a favour, but he dares not, he is hesitating, in fact, he is afraid that this is not the right moment, doesn't want to appear vulgar . . . Then he launches into it: The château is big, very big, and it has lots of outbuildings, and there's the little house in the park in particular, nobody living in it but quite charming, perfectly self-contained. The problem is the factory is doing well, too well almost, and needs more and more people, especially engineers and managers, but there is nowhere left to put them because, as anyone would agree, they cannot live among the workers, in the labourers' houses, no, rubbing up against people who sometimes sleep four to a bed, who drink cheap wine and swear, and breed like animals, never! And so an idea had come to him, the Director, just an idea . . . if the Prosecutor would agree, there was nothing to force him, of course, every man is his own master, but even so, if he agreed to let the little house in the park, The Factory and Directors would be extremely grateful, would pay a good price obviously, and would put up only the chosen few, only the right sort, polite, discreet, quiet under-managers, if not managers, and no children. Fat droplets of sweat seeped under the Director's paper collar and into his smart books. He stopped speaking, and waited, no longer even looking at Destinat, who had risen and stood gazing out over the park and the enfolding mist.

There was a long silence. The Director was just regretting his boldness when Destinat suddenly turned round and agreed. Just like that. In a voice that gave away nothing. The other man could hardly believe it. He bowed his head and stammered his thanks, backing out and disappearing before his host could change his mind.

Why did the Prosecutor agree? To get the man to go, to leave him to his silence once again? Or was it that he liked being asked for something, at least once in his life, that was not life or death?

It was sometime about '97 or '98. A long time ago now. The factory paid for the repairs to the little house in the park. The damp had eaten away at it like an old boat. Before then it had been used for storing anything and everything: crooked wardrobes, rat traps, rusted scythes as thin as crescent moons, blocks of stone, slates, a Tilbury open-topped carriage, abandoned toys, balls of string, garden tools, ragged clothes and loads of antlers and boars' heads, all long dead and stuffed. The old man had been a keen shooting man. His son who could not bear to see the mounted heads, (strange given his occupation), stowed it all away there, great heaps of it. The spiders had woven a fair few webs over it all, giving it an antique patina, a kind of mysterious Egyptian look, like an old sarcophagus. Once the major work was done, a decorator was brought from Brussels to put the finishing touches to the place.

The first tenant arrived as soon as it was ready. He lasted six months and then there was a second, then he left, and a third came, and then a fourth, and so on. People stopped counting. They came and went, staying less than a year, all very much alike. The locals gave them all the same name. 'Oh look, there goes the Tenant!' they'd say. They were good tall boys, still quite young, who lived quietly and never went out, never brought women back, obeyed the rules. Otherwise it was out at seven for the factory, back at eight having had dinner in what we all called the Casino – though no one ever played anything there! – a big place that they used as a kind of engineers' mess. Some of them occasionally ventured out into the park on a Sunday. Destinat said nothing, let it pass. He watched them from a window, waited until they had gone before taking his own walk and sitting down on a bench.

The years passed. Destinat's life seemed to follow an immutable pattern, between the law courts in V, the cemetery where he went to visit his wife's grave every week, and the château in which he lived, shut away, as if invisible, withdrawn from the world which gradually wove a suit of austere legend around him.

He grew older but he stayed the same, in appearance at least. The same bone-chilling seriousness, the silence, dense as a closing century. If you wanted to hear his voice, which was very soft, you had only to go to a trial. There were plenty of them. We get more crime round here than in most places, maybe because the winters are long and people get bored, or maybe because the summers are too hot and the blood boils in people's veins.

Juries did not always understand the Prosecutor. He had read so much, they so little. You got all kinds on those juries, but usually the lowest sorts: stale-smelling artisans and ruddy-faced peasants, dutiful civil servants, tattered priests who had risen before dawn to come in from tiny rural parishes, carters, worn-out labourers. They got to sit on the good side of the court, but so many of them could easily have ended up on the other, stiff as a ladder-backed chair between two whiskered police officers. And I'm sure they realised this in some way, deep down, without wanting to admit it, and that this was what made them so often vitriolic towards the man they had to judge, the man they could so easily have been. Their brother in misfortune or in spirit.

As soon as Destinat's voice was heard in the courtroom, every murmur ceased. It was as if the room pulled itself together, like a man standing before a mirror and smoothing down his shirt to make the collar stand up properly. Catching each other's eyes, a whole room holding its breath. It was into this hush that the Prosecutor would cast his words, cleaving the silence. He never had more than five sheets of paper with him, whatever the case, whoever the accused. His trick was quite simple. No hot air. Just a clinical dissection of the crime and the victim, and that was all. But that in itself was quite something. Not one detail was spared: usually, he followed the doctor's report like a bible. Just reading it out could be enough. His voice would linger on the most trenchant words. Not a single wound was omitted, not one little nick, not the least jagged detail of a severed throat or a slit belly. Suddenly the whole courthouse would see images appear, summoned from the very depths, images of evil and the terrible transformations it invokes.

It is often said that we fear what we do not know. I actually believe that fear is born when we learn one morning something we did not know the night before. That was Destinat's secret: casually tossing facts under unsuspecting noses, facts that the jury could not live with. The result was a foregone conclusion. He could ask for a man's head and they would give it to him on a silver platter.

After that it was lunch at Le Rébillon. 'One less to worry about then, eh, Monsieur le Procureur?' from Bourrache as he led him to his table, pulling out his chair in a stately manner. Destinat unfolded his cutlery, and clinked the flat of his knife against his glass. Judge Mierck greeted him silently, and Destinat returned the greeting in the same way. They sat less than ten metres apart, each at his own table, and never exchanged a word. Mierck had the table manners of an ogre, napkin knotted around his neck like a stable lad, fingers greasy with sauce, his eye already clouded by a few half bottles of Brouilly. The Prosecutor, on the other hand, was well-bred. He took his knife to the fish as if he were caressing it. Outside it would be raining, as Judge Mierck gulped down his pudding and Belle de jour snoozed by the hearth, lulled by tired limbs and dancing flames. The Prosecutor would linger for a moment, caught in the coils of a soft, sweet dream.

Somewhere, someone was sharpening a blade and erecting a scaffold.

I have been told that Destinat's talents and fortune could have taken him anywhere. Instead he stayed in our town all his life. In other words, nowhere. In other words, he stayed where the hubbub of life was heard only as distant music, until one fine day it came crashing down on our heads and went on to plague us in the most terrible way for four whole years.

The portrait of Clélia still hung in the hall of the château. Dressed for a light-hearted age that had now vanished, she smiled as the world sank into the abyss. As the years passed, the fading varnish warmed her pale cheeks. Every day Destinat passed more slowly before her, a little more careworn, a little dulled. The distance between them was growing. Death robs us of beautiful things, but preserves them. That is its power. We cannot fight it.

Destinat loved to watch time go by, doing nothing but sitting on a rattan couch by a window or on the bench on a little manmade hillock which in the spring was covered with anemones and periwinkles, watching the languid waters of the Guerlante and the busy little canal flow past. You could have taken him for a statue.

For years, I have been trying to understand, but I do not think I am any cleverer than the next man. I fumble, I get lost, go round in circles. In the beginning, before the *Affaire*, Destinat was just a name to me, an official position, a house, a fortune, a face I encountered two or three times a week and to which I would raise my hat. As for what went on behind the face, I had no chance of knowing! Since that time, having lived with his ghost for so long, he has become quite the old acquaintance, the companion in misfortune, a part of myself you could say, and one that I have tried to persuade to speak, tried to bring back to life so that I can ask it one question. Just one. Sometimes I tell myself that I am wasting my time, that the man was as impenetrable as the thickest fog, and that a thousand evenings with him would not be enough. But time is something that I have in plentiful supply. It is as if I have stepped outside the world. All the hustle and bustle is so far away now. I live in the wake of a story which is no longer my own. Bit by bit, I am bowing out.

U

1914. On the eve of the great massacre, there was suddenly a shortage of engineers. The factory was still just as busy, but for some unexplained reason the Belgians were keeping to their own little kingdom, under the frail protection of their carica-ture of a king. The Prosecutor was told, with much bowing and scraping, that there would be no more tenants.

The summer was promising to be as hot in the shade as it was in the overwound heads of many patriotic souls. People shook their fists and dusted down their painful memories. Wounds heal no more easily here than elsewhere, especially if left to grow raw and to fester through evenings of rancorous repetition. Thanks to pride and stupidity, one country was ready to throw itself into the jaws of another. Fathers urged on their sons, sons their fathers. Only the women – mothers, wives, sisters – had an inkling of suffering ahead, and saw clearly beyond those afternoons of gleeful shouting and wild toasts, of songs reverberating through the cloak of green foliage on the horse chestnut trees and ringing in everyone's ears.

Our little town heard the war but did not really join it. You could even be forgiven for saying that our town lived off the war. The men of the town kept the factory going. They were essential. An order came down from on high, a good one this time (which is pretty rare). Some distant bigwig, I forget who, issued a dispensation requisitioning the entire workforce for civilian service. Thus eight hundred good men escaped being blown to bits. Eight hundred men (if you could call them that, some thought) tumbled out of warm beds rather than muddy trenches every morning and went to push little trucks around, not corpses. What luck! The hurtling breath of exploding shells, the fear, the groans of dying friends caught on barbed wire twenty metres away, the carrion-fed rats, what did they know of that? Instead there was life. Real life. Life embraced every morning, not as a dream beyond the smoke but as a warm certainty that smelled of sleep and women. 'Lucky devils! Draft dodgers!' That's what the convalescing soldiers thought – the one-eyed, the legless, the amputees, the broken-limbed and mangled, the gassed and butchered – when they came across our healthy, rosy-cheeked factory workers with their lunch-bags. Some, with an arm in a sling or a wooden leg, would turn around as they passed and spit on the ground. You could understand why. People have hated for less.

Not everyone worked in the factory. The few remaining farm workers of the right age exchanged pitchforks for rifles. One or two set off proudly as cadets, not knowing that their names would soon be waiting to be engraved on a monument as yet unbuilt.

One man's departure stood out. This was the schoolmaster, a fellow with the improbably apt name of Fracasse, for he was to head off into that fracas. He was not from these parts, but a farewell ceremony was organised anyway. The children had composed a little song, something naïve and moving which brought a tear to his eye. The council gave him a tobacco pouch and a pair of fine gloves. I wonder what became of those delicate salmon-coloured gloves, which he took from the tissue paper in their shagreen leather box with an incredulous look. And what became of Fracasse himself: did he die, was he wounded, or did he make it through safe and well to the end?

He never came back here, anyway, and I understand that. The war killed thousands. It also carved our world and our memories in two, as if everything that happened before belonged to a better place, stowed in the depths of an old pocket where no one dared reach any more.

A replacement was sent, a man who was no longer eligible to be called up. The thing I remember most clearly about him were his eyes. They were like a madman's, two steely beads in oyster white. 'I'm an anti!' he told the mayor right off when he came to show him his class. So people called him the Anti. It's all very well being anti. But anti what? No one ever had any idea. Anyway, it was all over within three months. Though the fellow had probably been struggling for some time. Sometimes he would stop in the middle of a lesson and look up, making machine-gun noises with his tongue, or he mimed a shell falling to the ground, throwing himself on the floor and staying there, rigid, for ages, all alone with his anquish. Madness is never somewhere you go because you want to. Everything has to be earned. But at least he went there in style, lifting anchor and setting off with all the panache of a captain intent on scuppering his own ship.

Every evening he would slip along the canal, talking to himself, using words no one understood, stopping sometimes to strike some invisible foe with a hazel stick. Then he'd set off again, skipping along, going, 'Tagada Tagada Tsyong Tsyong!'

One day, when the artillery fire was very heavy, he went too far. Every five seconds the windowpanes quivered like water in a strong breeze, and the air was full of the smell of gunpowder and decaying flesh. Even the houses stank of it. We blocked up the cracks in the windows with damp cloths. Afterwards, the children told us how the Anti held his head in his hands for almost two hours, as if he was trying to hold it together, then he climbed onto his desk and started to take off his clothes quite methodically while singing the *Marseillaise* at the top of his voice. Then, naked as the day he was born, he ran all the way to the flagpole, pulled the flag down and peed on it before trying to set it alight. At this point, the young Jeanmaire boy, the oldest boy in the class at nearly fifteen, stood up calmly and stopped him with a mighty blow from a cast-iron poker across the top of his forehead.

'The flag! That's sacred!' the boy said proudly, when people gathered round to ask what happened. The flag was young Jeanmaire's birthright and he died three years later at the Chemin des Dames. Still for the flag.

When the mayor got there the schoolmaster was lying flat out, stark naked, on the red, white and blue, his hair singed by the pathetic excuse for a fire. Two male nurses led him away in a straitjacket which made him look as if he were going fencing, a purple bump on his head like a bizarre decoration. He was silent, like a little child who has just been told off. I think he was gone by that stage.

The fact remained that the school had no teacher and, although the children were not complaining, the authorities didn't like it. They sorely needed young soldiers turned out ready by the hundredweight. Particularly since by then the early illusions ('Don't worry about the Boches, we'll have taken Berlin in a fortnight!') had melted away, and no one knew how long it would all last. It seemed wise to provide some reserves. Just in case.

The mayor was tearing his hair out and pulling every string he could. It didn't help. He could neither find a solution nor a replacement for Fracasse.

Then the solution appeared all by itself, on 13 December 1914 to be precise, in a stagecoach from V. The coach usually stopped outside Quentin-Thierry's ironmongery with the window full of mole traps and boxes of mixed rivets. Four cattle merchants were seen getting off, all as red in the face as a cardinal's mitre, nudging each other and laughing out loud, having celebrated their deals a little too enthusiastically. Then two women got out, widows back from selling needlework at the crossroads. Then old Berthiet, a retired notary who went once a week to play bridge in a backroom at the Excelsior Grand Café with some other old has-beens. Then there were three young girls who had gone shopping for their trousseaus, and then, right at the end, when everyone thought there was no one left to come, we saw a young woman get off. A real ray of sunshine.

She looked right, then left, slowly, as if getting the measure of things. The bombardment had died down and the day still smelled slightly of autumn and bracken sap. At her feet were two little brown leather bags whose copper clasps seemed to secure secrets. She was dressed simply, no fuss or frills. She bent slightly, picked up her two bags and very slowly disappeared from sight, her slim silhouette enveloped by an evening haze of misty blue and pink.

She had a name, we learned later, in which a flower lay sleeping: Lilia. And this name fitted her like a ball-gown. She was not yet twenty-two, she came from the North, and was passing through. Her family name was Verhareine.

Her short walk took her to the little haberdasher's shop run by Augustine Marchoprat. The latter, at the young woman's request, told her where the *mairie* was and where the mayor lived. She had asked for the information, 'in a voice sweet as sugar', the local gossips would say later. And old mother Marchoprat, whose tongue was the size of an ox's, closed her door, pulled down the metal shutter and ran across the road to tell her old friend Mélanie Bonnipeau, a sanctimonious bigot in a bonnet who spent most of her time peering out of her ground-floor window between her fat cat and the aqueous limbs of her house plants as they unfurled against the panes. And the two old women began spinning possibilities, straying into novelette territory, overworking every episode and making it all even more overblown and ridiculous, until they were joined, about half an hour later, by Louisette, the mayor's maid – and the next thing to a goose.

'Well, who is she?' asked old mother Marchoprat.
    'Who is who?'
    'The girl with the two bags, stupid!'
    'She's from the North.'
    'From the North, which North?' the haberdasher persisted.
    'I don't know, the North, there aren't that many of them.'
    'And what does she want?'
    'She wants the job.'
    'What job?'
    'Fracasse's.'
    'Is she a teacher?'
    'That's what she says.'
    'What about the mayor, what does he say?'
    'Oh, he smiled at her very sweetly!'
    'Doesn't surprise me!'
    'He said: "You're saving my life!" '
    'You're saving my life!'
    'Yes, like I said.'
    'There's another one with ideas at the back of his mind!'
    'What sort of ideas?'
    'You poor girl! Ideas in his trousers then. You know what your master's like, he's a man!'
    'But you can't have ideas in trousers . . .'
    'God, she's stupid! And how did you get your little bastard then? From sitting in a draught?'

[31]

Louisette, a little put out, turned on her heel and left. The two old girls were satisfied. They had enough to keep them going for the evening, talking about the North, about men and their vices, about the young creature, who looked anything but a schoolteacher, who was definitely far, far too pretty to be a schoolteacher, pretty enough not to have to work at all.

The following morning we knew everything, or nearly everything.

Lilia Verhareine had spent the night in the largest room in the only hotel in town, at the expense of the town council. And the mayor, dressed like a young bridegroom, had come to collect her in the morning to introduce her to everyone and take her to the school. The poor man had to be seen to be believed, prancing about so much he nearly split his jasper black trousers, and – with him being so fat – looking about as graceful as a dancing elephant. And all for this young lady who was looking past it all, as if she were trying to project herself, lose herself, beyond it, at the same time shaking our hands with the merest flick of her slender wrist.

She went into the school and looked around the room as if it were a battlefield. It stank of peasant children. Ashes from the burned flag still lay on the floor. Upturned chairs made it look as if a wild party had just ended. We watched, noses against the windows. Someone had written the first lines of a poem on the blackboard:

They have surely felt the biting cold
On their naked hearts beneath the open stars
And death, half . . .

The verse stopped there. The Anti must have written it, and we all thought of his eyes and the gymnastic exercises he used to do, while by then he was lying – where? – on some flea-ridden mattress? Or shivering under cold showers and the purple flashes of electric shocks?

The mayor said a few words as he opened the door. He pointed out the flag, then stuffed his sausage fingers into the watch pocket of his silk waistcoat, self-importantly silent but occasionally casting dark glances in our direction, as if he wanted to say: 'What the hell are you lot doing here, and what the hell do you want? Leave us alone. Piss off!' But not one person left. We drank down the scene as if it were a glass of rare wine.

The young woman took a few small steps to the right, to the left, and arrived at the desks, still with exercise books and pens lying about. She leant over one, read a page, and we saw her smile. The golden gauze of her hair frothed against her bare neck like foam on a wave. Next she stopped by the ashes of the flag, then she picked up a couple of chairs, casually arranged some dried flowers in a vase, rubbed out the unfinished verses without hesitation, and smiled at the mayor. He was nailed to the spot by that twenty-year-old's smile, and less than fifteen leagues away men were bayonetting each other's throats and shitting their trousers at the same time, dying in their thousands every day, far from any woman's smile, dying on ravaged soil where even the idea of a woman had become a dream, a drunken dream, too beautiful an insult.

The mayor's fingers stroked his belly in a would-be elegant manner. Lilia Verhareine left the classroom, her footsteps as delicate as a dancer's.

The schoolmaster had always had lodgings above the school, in three neat little rooms which faced due south and had a fine view of the hillside and its blanket of vines and cherry trees. Fracasse had made them very comfortable. I spent a couple of awkward evenings there with him, chatting about one thing and another. The place had smelled of beeswax, leather-bound books, reflection and bachelorhood. Once the Anti came, no one visited. And no one had been in the room since he was carried away.

The mayor put the key in the lock, heaved the door open, surprised it was so difficult, went inside and quickly lost his beaming, tour-guide smile. I am making this up, putting scenes together and filling in gaps, but I believe I am hardly inventing because we saw it all on his face when he came back out, read it in the forehead beaded with sweat and surprise, in his breathless pallor. He gulped down great lungfuls of air, leaning against the wall all the while, like the good peasant that he still was, dabbing at his face with a large and not very clean checked handkerchief.

A long while later Lilia Verhareine also came blinking back out into the light, but she looked over at us and smiled. Then she knelt down to pick up two newly fallen conkers that sprang, gleaming and magnificently fresh from their husks. She rolled them together in her hand, closed her eyes and inhaled their brown scent, and walked quietly away. We ran up the stairs, elbowing each other in our hurry. Inside, it was like the apocalypse.

Nothing remained of the little apartment's former charm. Nothing. The Anti had devastated the premises methodically, and so meticulously that he had cut each book in the bookcase into tiny squares, one centimetre by one centimetre – Lepelut, a pen-pusher obsessed with details, measured them before our eyes. He had taken the furniture, piece by piece, and chipped away at it with his pen-knife until he had transformed the lot into a huge, ash blond heap of wood shavings. Piles of leftover food sat about, crawling with insects of every kind. Heaps of dirty washing lay like gruesome bodies on the floor, stripped of flesh and broken. And on the walls, on every wall, the warlike verses of *La Marseillaise* harangued us in delicately formed letters across the daisy and hollyhock-patterned wallpaper. The madman had written those verses, written them and rewritten them, like a demented litany, so that we felt trapped inside the vast pages of some hideous book. He had traced each letter with the tips of his fingers, dipped in his own shit which he had excreted into every corner of those rooms. Every single day that he had spent amongst us. Did he do it when his morning exercises were finished, or under the cannons' roar, close to the unbearable birdsong, the obscene fragrance of honeysuckle, lilac and roses, beneath the blue of the sky, against the sweet wind?

The Anti had had his war. With his razor, his pen-knife and his shit, he had drawn out his battlefield, dug out his trench and carved out his hell. He had screamed out his suffering before it swallowed him up.

Yes, the stench was atrocious and the mayor was just a little man, no courage or guts, less than nothing. But the young schoolteacher, now she was a lady. She came out of that apartment without shuddering, or judging. She looked up at the sky, great boulders of cloud and smoke scudding across it, picked up two conkers and stroked them as if stroking the forehead of a fevered madman, his ashen brow the colour of death, paled by so many deaths, such agonies, these stinking wounds gaping open for centuries . . . next to them the smell of shit is nothing, just the weak, insipid, sour smell of a living body – a *living* body – and it should not disgust us, nor shame and destroy us.

The fact remained, she could not live there. The mayor was dumbstruck. He was at the Café Theriex, and onto his sixth absinthe, which was going down like the five before it, without waiting for the sugar to dissolve, all in an attempt to recover from his close brush with the darkness within us all. The rest of us were still thinking of the madman's verses, his shredded filthy universe, shaking our heads and shrugging our shoulders and whistling aloud. Beyond the little window the eastern sky was turning dark, like inky milk.

Eventually, sleep and drink overcame the mayor, and the chair and table collapsed below him to general laughter. We had another round of drinks. The talk picked up again. Talk, talk, talk. And then someone, I don't remember who, says something about Destinat. And someone else, I don't remember who that was either, goes: 'That's where they should put the schoolteacher, on M. Le Procureur's estate, that house in the park, where the Tenant used to live!'

Everyone thought it was an excellent idea, not least the mayor, who said he had been thinking as much for a while. We nudged each other knowingly. It was late. The church clock struck twelve into the night. A shutter smacked against a wall. Outside, rain scuttled along the ground like a great river.

The following morning the mayor had abandoned his posturing and his finery. He wore heavy corduroy trousers, a woollen jacket, an otter-skin cap and hob-nailed boots, and his head was lowered. The morning coat and the swagger had been packed away. Lilia Verhareine had seen through him. No point now trying to look like a gay dog. Anyway, if he had gone to see the Prosecutor dressed as if he was going to a dance it would have turned the man against him right away – Destinat would have looked at him the way people look at a monkey in a suit.

The little teacher was still smiling her distant smile. Her dress was as simple as that first day, but in leafy, autumn colours, edged with Bruges lace which made her look grave, almost religious. As the mayor floundered through the mud, she stepped lightly, avoiding the puddles and furrows the rain had gouged in the road. It looked like a game as she skipped along, as if she was tracking some gentle animal over the sodden ground, and beneath her smooth young features you could still trace the impish child she had so recently been, slipping away from her hopscotch to steal cherries and redcurrants from somebody's garden.

She waited on the front steps of the château while the mayor went in alone to speak to Destinat. The Prosecutor received him in the lofty hall, ten metres high, standing on the cold black and white tiles of the entrance, a giant checkerboard for a game which began in the dawn of time, in which starving and wretched men are pawns to the rich and powerful warriors – minions kept at a distance but always the first to fall. The mayor poured out his request all at once, without dressing it up. He spoke with eyes lowered, examining the tiled floor and Destinat's elegant calfskin gaiters. He kept nothing back – the *Marseillaise* in shit, the whole apocalyptic horror of it – and explained the idea that had occurred to so many of us, especially to him, that the young woman could lodge in the house in the park. He stopped, stunned, like an animal that's run into park railings or an oak tree. The Prosecutor did not reply. He was looking through the stained and leaded panes of the front door at a slender figure walking quietly to and fro. Then he indicated that he wanted to see the young woman, and the door opened on Lilia Verhareine.

I could embroider this here, it would be easy to do so, but what would be the point? The truth is more powerful just as it is. Lilia walked in and held out a hand that was so tiny that Destinat did not at first see it, preoccupied as he was with her shoes, little summer shoes of black crepe and leather, toe and heel slightly muddy. This mud, which was more grey than brown, had left a sticky deposit on the tiles, tingeing the black squares white and the white squares dark.

The Prosecutor was famous for having shoes shinier than a Republican Guard's helmet, whatever the weather. A whole metre of snow could fall, or torrents of rain, the road surface could disappear under sludge, but this man's shoes would still be immaculate. I saw him buffing them once in the corridor outside the courtroom, when he thought no one was watching, and not far away, behind the mellowed walnut panelling, twelve men held another man's head in the balance. I saw contempt as well as horror in that little gesture of his that day.

And I understood a good many things about him from it. Destinat hated mess of any sort, even the most natural and earthly. The great muddy clodhoppers on the accused's feet or on the men and women he passed in the street – they nauseated him. By your shoes you were judged. So much hinged on the perfect polish, like a bald pate at the end of a sun-drenched summer. But a crust of dried mud, a film of travel dust, a wet stain in a hardened fold of leather . . .

But there, confronted with those little dirt-splattered shoes which had just reordered the marble checkerboard, and the rest of the universe along with it, it was a different matter: the world ground to a halt.

After a while, Destinat took the proferred hand in his own, and held it. And kept holding it.

'For an eternity,' the mayor told us later. 'And a long one at that! He wouldn't let go of it, kept it in his, and his eyes, if you'd seen them, they were no longer his, and even his lips, they were moving, wobbling, as if he wanted to say something, but nothing came out. Nothing. He was just staring at the little thing, eating her up, you'd think he'd never seen a woman, or not one like her anyway . . . I didn't know where to look! Well, you wouldn't, would you? It was like they weren't there, the two of them, they'd locked themselves away somewhere, lost in each other's eyes like that, because the girl wasn't blinking either, she just kept on smiling her pretty smile at him, wasn't embarrassed, or shy, head up, and the spare prick of course was me . . . I was looking round for something, anything, so that I didn't look like a peeping tom, and that's when I latched onto the big picture of his wife in that long dress. What else could I do? She was the one who took her hand back first, but she kept her eyes on him, and the Prosecutor looked at his, his hand I mean, as if it had been flayed. He didn't say anything for ages then he said "yes", just "yes". I don't know what happened after that.'

He probably knew full well, but it didn't matter any more. He and Lilia Verhareine left the château and Destinat stayed. For a long time. Right there on the same spot. Eventually he went heavily upstairs to his apartments; Old Gloomy told me he had never seen him quite so stooped before, so slow, so dazed. Destinat did not even reply when the old man asked whether everything was all right. He might have come back down into the hall that night though, into the half-light that didn't yield to the bluish phosphorescence of the street lamps, to convince himself of what he had seen, to look at the fine traces of mud on the black-and-white checkerboard, and then into his wife's distant eyes. She was smiling too, but her smile was in another time; it could not be illuminated by any sort of light, and seemed infinitely removed from him.

Strange days followed.

The war was still being fought, perhaps more fiercely than ever before: the roads became furrowed with an endless stream of ants that looked like men, their bearded faces greying, thinning. The artillery bombardment became continuous, day and night, and it punctuated our lives like a macabre clock, its large hands sweeping over the injured and the dead. The worst of it was that we got to the stage where we almost did not hear it. Every day we watched men pass, always going in the same direction; young men, on foot, heading for death but still believing they could outwit it. They smiled, thinking of something they did not yet know. Their eyes still sparkled with the life they had had. The sky was the last thing left that was bright and pure, oblivious to the evil and decay that spread across the earth below its arc of stars.

So the young teacher moved into the little house in the

grounds of the château. It suited her better than it had suited anyone else. She turned it into a treasure trove, as beautiful as she was herself, a place where the wind breezed in uninvited and wrapped itself round the pale blue curtains and the vases of wild flowers. She spent hours smiling, no one knew at what, by the window or on the bench in the park, a little morocco-bound book in her hands, her eyes fixed beyond the horizon, always beyond it, on some point which could not be seen. Or perhaps it could be seen only with the heart.

It did not take us long to adopt her. She knew how to charm everyone around her so easily, she even charmed this suspicious little town. Even those who could have been her rivals, by which I mean young girls on the lookout for husbands, were soon nodding hello to her, and she would nod back, always with the same lively grace.

The children stared open-mouthed, and this made her laugh, but never unkindly. The school was never so well attended or so happy. Men couldn't keep their sons back to help with odd jobs any more, for now every day spent away from their desks was like a long boring Sunday.

Every morning, Martial Maire, a simpleton who had lost half his head under an ox's hoof, left a little bunch of flowers outside her classroom door. When there were no flowers there would be a handful of beautiful grasses and herbs, trailing the minty odour of wild thyme and the sugary scent of lucerne. Occasionally, when he could find neither grasses nor flowers, he would leave some pebbles, carefully washed at the big fountain in the Rue Pachamort, and dried on the wool of his holey vest. He would be gone before she found his offering. Some women would have laughed at the halfwit; they'd have thrown away the grass and the pebbles. But Lilia Verhareine picked them up slowly, while the pupils lined up motionless in front of her, eyes on her pink cheeks and her amber-blonde hair; and she would hold these gifts in the palm of her hand, almost caressing them, and once in the schoolroom she would arrange the flowers or grasses in a little blue swan-shaped vase, and the pebbles on the edge of her desk. Martial Maire would watch from outside till she threw him a smile, and then he would run off. Once or twice, when she met him in the street, she would touch his forehead, rather as people do when soothing a fever, and the touch of her warm palm would be almost too much for him.

Quite a few people would have liked to have been in the halfwit's shoes. Maire was in the ideal position, it seemed to them. She tended him like a child and he was as attentive to her as a young fiancé. No one ever thought to laugh at them.

And Destinat? Now, that was something else. Something dark and impenetrable. Barbe knew him better than most and she told me about it years later, a very long time after. Long after the *Affaire*, long after the war. By then, everyone was dead, Destinat in '21, the others too, and there was nothing to be gained from raking over the ashes. But she told me all the same. It was late one afternoon, outside the little house she'd retired to – Old Gloomy had been run over by a cart in '23, never heard it coming. Barbe liked her bit of harmless gossip, and the cherry brandy she'd taken with her from the château by the jarful. These are her words:

'The minute that girl moved into the house, he changed, we felt it straight away. He started going for walks in the park, like a poor old bumblebee going for the honey pot. He used to walk round and round the house, come high wind or hail. Before that, he wouldn't have put a toe outdoors. When he came home from V he'd shut himself up in his study, or in the library, and I'd bring him a glass of water on a tray, never anything else, and he'd dine at seven. And so it went. But once that teacher was there the routine changed. He would come home earlier, and then he'd go out into the park and he'd sit down on the bench for ages, reading or staring at the trees. You'd see him at a window, peering out like he was looking for God knows what. As for his meals, well, that took the biscuit.

He'd never been a great eater, but now he hardly touched a thing. He'd wave his hand and I'd have to take the whole lot away again. You can't live on air and water! I kept thinking we'd find him in a heap in his room one day, passed out, collapsed! But nothing happened to him. His face grew gaunt, specially round the cheeks, and his lips even thinner, and they were never very generous in the first place. And he'd always been one for early to bed, but now he was up all night. I heard him, slow footsteps upstairs, long silences. I don't know what he was doing, brooding, dreaming, what else? On Sundays he always managed to come across the girl when she went out. He made it look like it was by chance, but it was all arranged. I used to see him waiting for the right moment, and then popping out just like that. She pretended not to notice, and I don't know whether she realised. She'd say a nice loud hello, all bright and clear, and then she'd carry on. He'd reply, but slowly, almost silently, and he'd stay there, rooted to the spot. He could stay there for a long time, as if he thought something was going to happen, I don't know what, and then he'd give up and go back.'

Night was falling around us, cattle lowing as they were brought in for the night, shutters rattling, as Barbe talked on. I could see the Prosecutor walking along the paths in the park, going over towards the river, looking up at the windows of the little house where the girl lived. There was nothing new about it, a man nearing death becoming entangled in love's net. The story was as old as the hills! The thing is, it only seems ridiculous to other people, and those people never understand anyway. Propriety is thrown to the wind. And Destinat, Destinat of the marble expression and icy hands, had been lured into the snare by a beautiful face and a hammering heart. It made him seem human, actually human.

[44]

Barbe also told me of a big dinner there had been one evening. Destinat had made her get out all the silverware, and spend hours ironing the linen napkins and embroidered table-cloths. A dinner for fifty? No. Just for two, the young school-teacher and himself. Just the two of them. At either end of a huge table. It was not Barbe who cooked the meal, but Bourrache, called in specially from Le Rébillon, and it was Belle de jour who waited at table, while Barbe brooded, Old Gloomy having long since gone to bed. The dinner went on till midnight. Barbe tried to find out what on earth they had to say to each other, and Belle de jour told her: 'They're just looking at each other, just looking at each other . . .' Barbe might have spared herself the trouble asking. She drank brandy with Bourrache, who woke her up in the morning as he was leaving. She had fallen asleep at the table. Bourrache had cleaned up and put everything away. There in his arms, wrap-ped up in a blanket and sleeping the sleep of the innocent, was his daughter, Belle de jour.

By this point in her story, night was upon us, and the old servant fell silent and wrapped her shawl around her head. We stayed there together like that for a long time in the dark, without speaking, and I thought about what Barbe had been telling me. Then she rummaged in the pockets of her old apron as if she were looking for something. Up in the sky there was a mass of shooting stars, a ridiculous disjointed stream of them, an omen to comfort the lonely, and then everything settled down. What had been bright continued to shine, and what was concealed in darkness seemed even more obscure.

'Here,' Barbe said, 'perhaps you'll know what to do with this.' She handed me a large key.

'Nothing's been changed there since I stopped going. His only heir is a distant cousin on the wife's side, so distant no one's ever even seen him. The lawyer said he was in America.

I'd be amazed if he ever came back, and it would take ages to find him. Even the thought of it! . . . I won't be here much longer . . . You'll have to be the caretaker now, if you get my meaning.'

Barbe stood up slowly, closed my hand over the key, and then she went into her little house, without another word. I put the key to the château in my pocket and left.

I never had another chance to talk to Barbe. And yet I often felt the desire to, a bit like when you have a scab and it itches but you like it all the same. I kept thinking there was plenty of time. We all make that mistake: we think we have time, we can do it tomorrow, in three days, next year, in two hours' time. And then everyone dies. And we are left to walk behind coffins, which makes conversation difficult. At the graveside, I looked at Barbe's coffin and hoped it would give me some answers, but it was just a bit of wood, well polished of course, with the priest twirling his censor and his Latin phrases round it. Walking to the graveyard with the rest of the bleating little herd, I wondered whether Barbe had been leading me on with her stories of dinners and Destinat the Great Lover. Did it matter any more? The brandy or maybe the cherries had got the better of her. I hoped she would find great jars of it up there, amongst the clouds.

I still had the key to the château in my pocket and I had not once made use of it since that evening six months before. The sound of dirt being shovelled brought me back to earth. The grave was soon filled in and Barbe and Old Gloomy were together again, for a whole slice of eternity. The priest left with his two altar boys, their clogs slapping against the mud. His flock scattered like starlings over a field of green wheat and I went to visit Clémence's grave, slightly ashamed I didn't go more often.

The sun, the rain and the years had faded the photograph in

[46]

its porcelain frame. All I have is the shadow of her hair and, I can just make out the outline of her smile, as if she were looking at me from behind a veil. I put my hand on the gold letters of her name, and leave, and in my head I tell her all the little things that have made up my life, my long life without her, things that she must know well, having heard me go over them so many times.

It was later that day, in fact, after Barbe's funeral, that I decided to go to the château. I wanted to return to that mystery to which I was now one of the last witnesses. Yes, that was the day I cleared away the brambles which had grown like stubble around the door, and I slid the key into the lock, like a threadbare prince forcing his way into the palace of a sleeping beauty. Except that there, behind that door, nothing really slept any more.

ix

There is something else I want to say before I tell you about the château in its dust and shadows. I want to talk about Lilia Verhareine, because I saw her, as everyone did. Our town is not large, paths cross. Every time I met her, I raised my hat. She returned my greeting with a lowered head and a slight bow. But one day I saw something different in her eyes, something sharp, cutting, like a spray of gunshot.

It was on a Sunday, in the lovely early evening, in the spring of 1915. The air smelt of apple blossom and acacia flowers. I knew that every Sunday the little teacher took a walk, following the same path to the top of the hill. She didn't care whether the sun was shining or the rain was bucketing down. I knew that.

I used to hang around there too, with a small shotgun I had been given by Edmond Gachentard, an old colleague who had gone to plant cabbages or something in the Caux, and to look after his wheelchair-bound wife. That shotgun was a pretty, feminine little thing, just the one barrel gleaming like a new coin, and a cherrywood butt on which Gachentard had had these words engraved: *'You will feel nothing.'* The phrase was intended for the game he hunted, but Gachentard was afraid it might apply to his wife and all of a sudden he couldn't bear it any more, looking at her dead legs and colourless face. 'You'd better have it,' he said one evening, handing it to me wrapped in a newspaper which bore the crumpling image of the Queen of Sweden. 'Do what you like with it . . .'

That was an odd thing to say, and I mulled over those words for a long time. What could you actually do with a shotgun? Grow chicory, play music, go to a dance, darn socks? A shotgun is for killing. It has no other use. I have no taste for blood. But I took the thing, thinking that if I left it with Edmond I might, unintentionally, have murder on my conscience, a little drink-fuelled murder, well out of sight but even so . . . Since then, I have got into the habit of taking the gun with me on my Sunday strolls, using it almost as a walking stick. Over the years, the barrel has lost its sheen and gone a shadowy grey, which suits it well enough. The words Gachentard had engraved have more or less disappeared, all that you can read are the *You* and the *nothing*: '*You . . . nothing*,' prophetic and dispiriting.

Edmond Gachentard had big feet, a Basque beret and a devastating weakness for complicated apéritifs, which smelled so strongly of plants they could have been mistaken for herbal remedies. He would often look up at the sky and shake his head, and become thoughtful when fat clouds tarnished that pure blue with white. 'Bastards . . .' he'd say, but I was never sure whether this applied to the clouds or to something else, lost to view, which only he could discern up there. That is what I think of when I think of him. Memory is a strange thing: it holds onto things that have no value at all. And buries the rest. Gachentard must be buried now. Or one hundred and five years old. His middle name was Marie. Another piece of information for you. This must stop. No more.

When I say no more, that is what I mean. What is the point of all these words, these lines huddled like geese in winter, these words stitched together without any obvious pattern? The days go by, and I sit down here at my table. I can't say I enjoy it, but I can't say that I don't.

Yesterday Berthe, who comes to push dust around three times a week, came across one of the notebooks, the first I think. 'Well I never,' she said, 'You do waste a lot of paper!' I looked at her. She's stupid, but no more than most. She carried on with her chores without waiting for a reply, singing the foolish songs she's kept in her head since she was twenty and looking for a husband. I would have liked to explain it to her, but explain what? That I keep on going down the lines of the page as if they are roads through an unknown and yet familiar land? I gave up. And when she left I went back to work. The worst of it is that I could not care less what happens to these notebooks. I am onto the fourth now. I don't know where to find the second or the third. I must have lost them, or Berthe must have taken them for firelighters. Does it matter? I don't want to read them. I write. That's all. It's almost as if I was talking to my-self, having a conversation with myself, a conversation that began in another time. I am packing the family portraits away. I am digging graves without dirtying my hands.

On that particular Sunday I had been walking over the hillside for hours. Some way below me lay the town, gathered in on itself, the houses packed hard against each other, and further back the great mass of the factory with its brick chimneys reaching up into the sky as if they were going to poke it in the eye. A vista of smoke and labour, a sort of cara-pace with masses of little snails inside it, all quite blissfully oblivious of the rest of the world and self-contained. And yet the world was not far away – you only had to climb the hill to see it. That's probably why families on their Sunday walks preferred the drab safe banks of the canal, with only the occasional slap of a fat carp to ruffle the waters, or the prow of a barge. The hill was like a curtain, concealing a stage, but no one wanted to see the performance. We are cowards, if we are allowed to be. If the hill had not been there, the war would have ploughed right into us, like a real, undeniable reality. But, as it was, we managed to pretend that it wasn't happening, despite the racket that came at us like shit out of a man with diarrhoea. The war performed delightfully on the other side of the hill, a good way away, in other words nowhere, in other words, in another world which bore no relation to this world of ours. No one wanted to go and look. We made a myth of it. That is how we managed to live with it.

That Sunday I had climbed higher than usual, not much higher, just a few dozen metres, almost by accident. I was fol-lowing a thrush one step at a time as it fluttered and cheeped, dragging a broken and blooded wing behind it. I was so busy watching the bird that I eventually reached the ridge, which is only a ridge in name, because the hill is actually crowned by a large meadow which makes it look like a huge hand, palm up, covered in grass and stumpy little copses. I felt a warm wind blow against my neck, and felt, knew somehow, that I had overstepped the line, that invisible line that those of us who lived down below had drawn on the ground, and in our heads. I looked up, and saw her.

She was sitting right ahead of me, quite happily, on the grass dotted with daisies, and the pale fabric of her dress spreading out from her waist reminded me of those rural idylls painters are so fond of depicting. The wildflower meadow seemed to have been arranged for her alone. Every now and then the breeze lifted the tiny foaming curls which shadowed her neck. She was looking straight ahead, watching what we would not see, what we did not want to see. A lovely smile played on her face, a smile which made the ones she gave us every day, and God knows they were beautiful enough, seem paltry and aloof. She was looking at that wide plain, that brown endless plain that rippled through the distant smoke of explosions whose fury was spent by the time they reached us, no longer real, in fact.

In the distance the front line blurred the horizon, so that every now and then it looked as if many suns were rising all at once, only to fall back to the sound of an abortive detonation. The war played out its manly game across many kilometres, and from where we were, you could have been forgiven for thinking it was a special production performed by circus dwarves, everything was on a miniature scale. Death itself was diminished. And with it went the whole kit and caboodle of suffering, tragedy, of mangled bodies and unheard screams, of fear and hunger in a thousand bellies. Lilia Verhareine watched it all with eyes wide open. In front of her, on her lap, she had what I at first thought was a book, but after a moment, she started writing in it, and I saw quite clearly that it was in fact the little morocco-covered notebook. She wrote a few words with a pencil so small it was swallowed up by her hand, and as she put those words on the page, her lips shaped other words, or perhaps they were the same. I felt somehow like a thief, watching her like that, from behind.

I was just thinking this to myself when she turned around, slowly, leaving her beautiful smile on the distant battlefield. Like the idiot I was, I stayed there, bolt upright, not knowing what to say or do. If I had been stark naked I couldn't have felt more embarrassed. I tipped my head. She went on looking at me, and for the first time I saw her face smooth as a lake in winter, the face of a dead woman. I mean the face of a woman who had died inside, and nothing about her was alive any more, nothing moved, the blood itself had left her.

It went on and on, like torture. Then her gaze fell from my face to my left hand, where Gachentard's shotgun hung limp. I saw what she saw and I went as red as a woodpecker's arse. I stammered a few words which I immediately regretted: 'It's not loaded, it's just to . . .' then I stopped myself. Could I have been more stupid? I should have shut up. She did not take her eyes from me. It was like having nails dipped in vinegar driven into my flesh, then she shrugged her shoulders and turned back to her view, leaving me to flounder in this world that was too ugly for her, too crowded, too suffocating. The immortals know nothing of this world, but they might tiptoe through it sometimes on their way. This world of mere men.

After that Sunday I did my best to avoid her. Whenever I spied her in the distance, I hurtled down side streets, fell into doorways, hid under my hat if there was nothing else. I never wanted to see her eyes again. I could not shake off that terrible feeling of shame. And yet, when I thought back to it, I couldn't understand it! What had I actually seen? A young woman alone, writing in a red notebook as she watched a scene of war. And I had just as much right as her to go wandering through the meadows if I felt like it!

I hung the shotgun on a nail above my door. It's still there. It was not until everyone was dead and buried that I resumed my Sunday walks. I would go back each time, as if on a pilgrimage, to that part of the meadow where I had seen her, sitting on the edge of our world.

I always sit where she sat, on the exact spot, and catch my breath for a while. I look at what she was looking at, the wide vista now languorous and calm once more, no flashes or plumes of smoke, and I still see the smile she gave that glorious, war-splattered infinity, I still see it all, as if the scene is going to be played over once again, and I wait. I wait.

And still the war went on. Those who boasted that it would only take three weeks and two shakes of a lamb's tail for the Boches to be sent back home with a kick up their backsides were not so cocky now. No one celebrated the first anniversary of the fighting, except Fermillin, a great thin man with a wet blanket of a face, who had spent ten years on the Northern Railways before discovering his real 'calling', as he put it, was the selling of liquor.

Fermillin ran a bistro called Au Bon Pied, which meant precious little in the context of a bar, as people had pointed out many times. He replied, rather tartly, that he knew why it was called that, even if no one else did, and they could all go to hell as far as he was concerned.

After he'd bought everyone a round, we all agreed with him and most of us even decided that Au Bon Pied was not that bad a name after all: it had a bit of a ring to it, distinctive you might say, and it made a change from all the Excelsiors, Florias, Terminuses and Cafés des Amis. And it made you thirstier.

On 3 August 1915 Fermillin unfurled a big banner made of old sheets with the words, in red, white and blue: '*One year on! Glory to our heroes!*'

Celebrations got under way towards five in the afternoon. There were all the regulars: Old Voret, a fat and happy widower now retired from the factory; Janesh Hiredek, a Bulgarian immigrant who spoke French badly when he was sober but could quote Voltaire and Lamartine after a couple of litres of wine; Léon Pantonin, always knows as Green Face after being a guinea pig for a new copper-oxide treatment for pneumonia; Jules Arbonfel, a giant of a man who looked like a monkey but had a voice like a girl; and Victor Durel, whose wife would come to Au Bon Pied looking for him and three hours later had to be carried home herself.

The bistro shook till three o'clock in the morning to the vigorous echo of all the great old fighting songs, a tremor in the voice bringing tears to the eye; over and over again they rang out. The noise got worse whenever the door opened and one of the combatants came out to pee under the stars, before going back into the jaws of that wine-fuelled monster. In the morning there was still the odd groan escaping from the place and an indefinable stench of stale wine, blood, old shirts, sick, and cheap tobacco. Most of the revellers had slept there. Fermillin, first to get up, shook them awake like plum trees before giving them a breakfast of pinot blanc.

I saw Lilia Verhareine go past the café, and smile, as Fermillin gave her a deep bow and laid it on with his *Mademoiselle*. I saw her, but she did not see me. I was too far away. She was wearing a dress the colour of a hothouse peach and a little straw hat with a deep red ribbon on it, and she had a large plaited bag swinging cheerfully on her hip. She was heading towards the fields. It was 4 August. The sun was shooting up like an arrow and already the dew was disappearing. The heat promised to fan every kind of desire. We could not hear the artillery. Even if we strained, we could not hear it. Lilia turned the corner by the Mureaux' farm and set off into open countryside where the earth lay sleeping, succumbing to the scents of cut hay and ripe wheat. Fermillin was still on the doorstep of his bistro, rubbing his rough chin, reddened eyes lost in the sky. A gaggle of boys set off exploring, pockets bulging with sandwiches. Women hung sheets on lines, and they billowed in the wind. Lilia Verhareine disappeared. In my mind's eye, I saw her walking along the summer paths as if they were avenues of sand.

I never saw her again.

I mean I never saw her alive again. That very evening, the Marivelle boy ran all the way over to my house, catching me stripped to the waist and pouring a pitcher of water over my head. Water ran down his cheeks too, great fat tears like streams of wax, making his young face swell up as if he had been standing too close to a furnace.

'Come quickly, come quickly!' he said. 'Barbe sent me. Come to the château. Quickly!'

The château. I knew the way well enough: I left the boy standing and set off like a rabbit, thinking I was going to find Destinat with his throat slit, his belly cut open by some disgruntled convict back to present his compliments after twenty years roasting in a penal colony. As I hurried along the path, I was already telling myself that, when all was said and done, it would serve him right. That's how he should end his days, I was thinking, taken by surprise by some barbarous killer, because in amongst all those heads he'd sent rolling there must have been one or two innocents, carried bodily to the scaffold, still protesting, immaculate as the Virgin herself.

And so I arrive at the open gate, my hair damp, my shirt untidy, my trousers buttoned up all wrong and my heart pounding. And suddenly on the doorstep, as alive as I am myself, very much on his feet, as collected as the devil, as cool as a Swiss guard, I see M le Procureur, with his entrails still in their proper place and his blood still in his veins. And seeing him there like that, rigid as a ship's mast, hands clutching at nothing, eyes looking into the distance, mouth slack and trembling, it suddenly occurs to me – if not him, then . . . who? And all at once I see Lilia Verhareine once again, turning the corner at the Mureaux' farm, I see the scene over and over again, more real than real, all the details, the way her dress moved, her little bag swinging, her neck white under the burgeoning sun, the ring of the anvil in Bouzie's forge a few steps away, the red of Fermillin's eyes, every sweep of old Madame Sèchepart's broom on her front step, the smell of fresh straw, the swifts plaintively piping over the roofs, the cattle lowing as the Dourin boy herds them over to the meadow. All of it, ten times, a hundred times, as if I cannot escape, as if I have locked myself into this scene for ever.

I do not know how long we stayed like that on the threshold, facing each other without seeing each other, the Prosecutor and myself. I no longer know how it all fitted together. It's not that my memory now has gaps in it, more that the moment itself was never whole. I was like a robot, following him mechanically. Did he lead me, take my hand? Who knows! After a bit I began to feel alive again, felt blood pounding in my chest. My eyes were open. The Prosecutor was beside me, behind and to the left of me. We were in a light room filled with vases of flowers. There was a chest of drawers, a wardrobe, a bed.

And on the bed lay Lilia Verhareine. Her eyes were closed. Closed to the world and to all of us. Her hands were drawn up to her chest and she was wearing the dress she had worn that morning, the colour of a hothouse peach, and the little shoes in that indefinable shade of dusty terracotta. There was a moth fluttering above her, like a madman, flapping against the half-open window, and setting off all the more frantically in its lurching circles towards her face, only to thud into the window again, as if dancing some hideous pavane.

[57]

The collar of the girl's dress was open so that I could see traced on her throat a deep furrow of red so dark it was almost black. The Prosecutor glanced up at the ceiling and the blue porcelain lamp, flanked by a counterweight in the form of a globe (gleaming copper, five continents, seas and oceans), then he took from his pocket a belt of fine plaited leather, decorated with daisies and mimosa, which a slender, once supple hand had formed into a loop: a perfect circle, like a philosophical image, promise and fulfilment, beginning and end, birth and death.

At that point, we said nothing to each other. We looked at each other: yes, our eyes sought each other, before quickly sliding back to the young schoolteacher's body. Death had not robbed her of her beauty, not yet. She was still amongst us, you could say, her face nearly alive, her skin pale, and when I laid my hands on hers they were still warm. That shocked me. I expected her to open her eyes, to look at me, to protest against the liberty I had taken with her. Then I buttoned the collar of her dress so that the fabric might hide the line of bruising, and conceal the true nature of her sleep.

The Prosecutor did not stop me. He made not one movement, took not one step, and when I looked away from Lilia and back into his bewildered eyes I saw that they were asking me a question, a question to which I had no answer. Dear God, what did I know about death? What do I know even now? It was more his department than mine, after all! He was the specialist. He'd asked for it so often, he was on such familiar terms with it, he met it several times a year, for God's sake, in the prison yard when one of his victims was being trimmed by a head or so before lunch at Le Rébillon!

Nodding towards the belt, I asked whether he had . . . ? 'Yes,' he said before I had time to finish. I cleared my throat and said: 'Did you find anything?' He looked around slowly, taking in the wardrobe, the chair, the chest of drawers, the dressing table, the vases of flowers like fragrant sentries, the dense hot night pressing against the window, the bed, the curtain, the bedside table on which lay a delicate watch, whose impatient hands urged time on, then he looked back at me. 'Nothing . . .' he said, distraught, not like himself at all, and I could not be sure whether it was a statement or a question, or the words of a man who felt the ground beneath his feet shifting and sliding away.

I heard footsteps on the stairs, slow and reluctant. Barbe and Old Gloomy came in with Hippolyte Lucy, the doctor, a good man, thin as a rake, kind and very poor – the two things went together, for he rarely charged the poor for his services and most of our town was poor. 'You can pay me later!' he'd say with a golden smile. 'I'm not destitute,' he would add under his breath. And yet it was destitution that killed him, in '27. 'Died of starvation!' said Desharet, the fat fool, he of the garlic breath and ruddy complexion, when he came over from V, in his shiny car to examine his colleague's brittle stick of a body which someone had found on the floor of his kitchen, his kitchen with nothing in it, no furniture, no food, not a crust of bread, not a knob of butter, just a plate which had lain empty for days on end, and a glass of well water. 'Died of starvation,' went the bastard in an offended tone, all dressed up in flannel like an Englishman, his own belly and jowls dragging along the floor. 'Starvation . . .' He couldn't get over it. If we had dunked his head in a bucket of slurry he couldn't have been more astonished.

Doctor Lucy went up to Lilia but he did not do much. What was there to do? He put his hand on the girl's forehead, let it slide down to her cheeks, her throat, and as soon as he saw the furrow he stopped. All we could do was stand looking at each other, our mouths hanging open on all the questions which would never be asked. Barbe let us know there was nothing more for us to do in this young girl's room, which now would remain so for ever. One look from her and we left, obedient as children, Old Gloomy, the doctor, the Prosecutor and me.

Of course the war went on, and on, and it had already produced more corpses than you could count. But still the news of the young teacher's death came as a shock to the town. The streets were deserted. The gossips, old magpies, usually so ready to speak ill of anyone, held their tongues at home. In the bars men drank silently; the only sound was of glasses, bottles, throats, being emptied. Nothing else. Was it a tribute to her, or were they just stunned? Even the summer seemed to be at half-mast. There were some grey days, suffocating days when the sun did not dare show itself and hid behind great dark clouds, the colour of mourning. Children no longer hung about on the streets, or went fishing, or threw stones at windows. Even the animals seemed to have lost their will. The church bells chopped up time like the trunk of a dead tree. Only Martial Maire, the simpleton who understood perfectly, howled his grief, huddled in the school doorway, baying like a wolf. Perhaps we should all have done the same. Perhaps it was the only thing to do.

I should have questioned the Prosecutor. That is the form when there is a violent death. Or, let's call a spade a spade, a suicide. Yes, I should have questioned him. It was my job. But I did not. What would have been gained by it? Nothing, probably. I would have stood in front of him like a fool, fiddling with my cap and looking at the floor, the ceiling, my hands, not daring to ask the right questions, and what would the right questions have been anyway? He was the one who found her. He had been out walking, had noticed the open window, looked in and saw the body. He had run in, forced the lock of the bedroom door, and then . . . and then? Nothing. He had taken her in his arms, had lain her down on the bed. Had called for me. That much he did say, after Barbe had sent us out and we were wandering about the lawn, not knowing where to go or what to do.

In the days that followed, Destinat stayed out of sight in his château. Barbe told me, that night when she told me everything, that he spent all his time at the window, looking over at the little house as if the young schoolteacher might still come out. The mayor and I tried to find out whether Lilia Verhareine had any family. We found nothing, just a scored-out direction on some envelopes, which turned out to be the address of a former landlady. The mayor spoke to her on the telephone, but he could only catch every second word because of her northern accent. Nevertheless, he did gather that the landlady knew nothing. When letters came, the landlady put the new address on them, the one the young lady had sent her. 'Were there a lot of letters?' I heard the mayor ask. But at that point the line was cut and we got no reply. There was a war on, and even the telephone was at war in its way.

So we spoke to Marcel Crouche, the postman, who never managed to finish his rounds because of the other sort of rounds which he never turned down: glasses of wine, little drops here and there, rum in his coffee, Pernods and Vermouths. By late morning he'd be slumped against the washhouse wall spouting political clap-trap and then snoring to his heart's content, postbag clamped tightly in his arms. The château was towards the end of his round, by which time he was usually staggering like a sailor on high seas. 'Letters? Of course there are letters for the château, but I look at the address, not the name. When it says château I deliver to the château, and that's all! Whether it's for the Prosecutor or for the young lady, I'm buggered if I know. I hand everything over and he's the one who sorts them out. I always give them straight into his hands, never to Barbe or Old Gloomy, he makes a point of it, the Prosecutor does, I mean it's his house, isn't it?'

Marcel Crouche buried his great pockmarked nose into his glass of brandy, inhaling as if his life depended on it. The three of us, the mayor, the postman and myself, drank in silence. Then there was another round. The mayor and I looked at each other over our glasses, and we knew what we were both thinking. But we also knew that neither of us would dare to go and ask the Prosecutor. So we said nothing. Not another word.

The Education Department was no more helpful. All they could say was that Lilia Verhareine had volunteered for a post in our region. I was made to wait three-quarters of an hour in the corridor outside the inspector's office in V in order to feel the full weight of the man's importance, and the inspector seemed more interested in smoothing down his moustache than in the young schoolteacher. He mispronounced her name several times, made a pretence of leafing through some files, consulted his beautiful gold watch, flattened his hair with his hand and inspected his clean fingernails. He had eyes like a calf, utterly blissfully stupid, like the poor creatures who are led to their deaths without a single sob because they cannot imagine such a mystery. He called me *My dear chap* but, coming from him, it was dispensed so haughtily that it sounded as if he were swearing.

After a while he rang for someone, but no one came. So he shouted. Still no one. He started bellowing, and a sickly face like a washed-out turnip appeared, coughing in a doomed way every thirty seconds, as if announcing that all good things come to an end. This was Mazerulles, the inspector's secretary. The Inspector hurled his name as if he were cracking a whip. Mazerulles did genuinely try to rake back through his memory, though. And he remembered the girl, and the day she came. Appearances can be deceptive. Mazerulles looked like a larva, a halfwit, a weakling, not someone you would depend on. His flaccid body seemed to fit together rather badly. But then I started to talk to him about the girl, and I told him what had happened. If I had hit him between the eyes with a truncheon it could not have stunned him more. He leant against the doorframe and stammered unintelligibly, about youth, beauty, waste, war, the end. It was just us then, Mazerulles and me, with a little ghost gradually forming between us in every word we exchanged.

The Inspector could feel it too, imbecile that he was, hopping about behind us, and breathing heavily: 'Right, right, right,' as if he wanted to get rid of us as soon as possible. I left the office with Mazerulles, without a word of goodbye to the stuffed shirt. The door slammed on us and we ended up in the secretary's office. It was very small, very like him, quite pitiful and uncomfortable. It smelt of wet clothes and firewood, and of menthol too, and coarse tobacco. He offered me a chair next to the stove, and sat down at his desk where three squat little inkpots were enjoying a rest. Then he pulled himself together and told me about the day Lilia Verhareine had come to the office. I learned nothing new, but I derived some pleasure from hearing someone talk about her, someone not from our town. We had not been dreaming. She really had existed. This man I did not know from Adam was describing her to me. When Mazerulles had finished I shook his hand, wished him good luck, I am not sure why, it came to me just like that, but he did not seem surprised. He simply said: 'Oh, luck and me, well, you know . . .' I did not know, but I could guess by looking at him.

What can I say now? Should I describe Lilia Verhareine's funeral? It was a Wednesday. The day was as beautiful as the day she had chosen to leave us. Perhaps even hotter. Yes, I could tell you about that, about the sun, the children with their homemade garlands of vine leaves and wheat, the church packed full: Bourrache with his little daughter, the Prosecutor right at the front like the chief mourner, the fat new priest, Father Lurant, whom we had not yet quite accepted until somehow he managed to voice exactly what so many of us felt in our hearts, and performed this service as if it were the most natural thing in the world. Yes, I could describe all that, but I will not.

The thing that changed, that really changed, was the Prosecutor. He still went on calling for people's heads, but his heart was no longer in it. Worse, he sometimes seemed to get completely confused during his summing-up. No, that's not strictly true. A better way to explain it would be to say that, when he was listing the facts and drawing his conclusions, he sometimes ground to a halt, gazed into the middle distance and stopped talking. As if he wasn't there, on his high perch in the law courts, as if he was somewhere else. As if he had gone. Oh, they never lasted very long, these absences, and no one thought to tug at his sleeve to set him on the right track again. When he went back to his summing-up, everyone seemed relieved, even the fellow being tried.

The Prosecutor had the little house in the park locked up. There were no more tenants. And there were no more school-masters until the end of the war. Destinat stopped taking walks in the park. He went out less and less. We learned a little later that he had paid for the coffin and the gravestone. We all thought it a handsome gesture on his part.

A few months after the teacher died, I learned from Léon Schirer – who was a sort of general dogsbody at the law courts in V – that Destinat had asked to take retirement. Schirer was not the sort to lie, but even so I had trouble believing him. Firstly because the Prosecutor, although he was no longer young, still had a good few years ahead of him. And secondly, I wondered what on earth he would do in retirement, other than get monumentally bored, all alone in that house big enough for a hundred people, with two servants he hardly addressed three words to in a day.

I was wrong. Destinat delivered his last summing-up on 15 June 1916. He spoke without conviction, and he did not, in fact, obtain the defendant's head. Once the courtroom was empty, the presiding judge gave a short speech, and then everyone had a little drink. The judges were all there, headed up by Mierck, the lawyers, the clerks and a few others. I was there too. Afterwards, everyone went to Le Rébillon for a farewell meal. I say everyone, but I was not among them. It was fine to have a glass of cheap champagne with me, but when it came to the kind of things you could only savour if you had been born to them, well I could forget about it.

Then Destinat withdrew into silence.

xii

Let's go back now to that morning in 1917 when we left Belle de jour's body beside the frozen canal, along with Judge Mierck and his devoted retinue.

This must all seem a terrible muddle, hopping shambolically from one thing to the other, but that's how my life has been, little snippets chopped up and impossible to stitch back together again. To understand someone, you have to dig right down to the roots, right down into the cracks, drag it up and let the poison seep out. Get your hands dirty. Nothing disgusts me – I'm just doing my job. Outside, there is darkness, and what can I do in the dark but get the same old sheets out again and again, and darn them a little more?

Mierck still wore the haughty look of a gout-ridden ambassador, gobbets of egg-yolk still stuck in his moustache. He looked at the château and a laugh lingered at the corners of his mouth. The little door was open, and in places the grass had been trampled. The judge started whistling quietly and swinging his shooting stick as if it were a fly-swat. The sun had broken through the mist and was melting the frost. We were frozen stiff as fenceposts, our cheeks hard as the soles of our shoes. Crusty had stopped taking notes – what was he taking notes of anyway? It had all been said. 'Good, good, good . . .' Mierck began again, rocking on the balls of his feet.

Then he swung sharply round on the local policeman: 'Give

[67]

him my compliments!' he said. The poor man was completely flabbergasted: 'Give your compliments to who, your honour?' Mierck looked at him as if he was a peabrain. 'To who? To whoever cooked my eggs, my friend! They were excellent! Who do you think? Pull yourself together!' The policeman saluted. Judge Mierck had a way of calling people *my friend* while meaning the reverse. He had a way of using words, making them say things they were never meant to say.

We could have stayed like that a lot longer, the judge, the policeman (of boiled egg fame), Crusty, young Bréchut, Grosspeil, Berfuche and myself – as usual, the judge had still not spoken to me. The doctor had been and gone with his leather bag and his kid gloves, leaving Belle, or rather the girlish shape of Belle, under the wet blanket. The bustling waters of the canal flowed on. I was reminded of a Greek saying, although I did not recall it exactly, about time and water flowing, a few simple words which said everything there was to say about life. Or at least making it clear that you could never go back upstream, in life, that is. However much you tried.

Two ambulance men eventually came breezing in, soon feeling the cold in their thin white overalls. They had come over from V and had gone round in circles for some time before finding us. The judge nodded to them and pointed at the blanket: 'Take it!' You'd have thought he was talking about an old nag, or a table in a restaurant. I left, without speaking to anyone.

But I had to go back, back to the water's edge. I had to do my job, as well as my duty, which is no easier. I waited till the early afternoon, till the bitter nip of morning was past. And it was almost mild, a different day, you might have thought. Grosspiel and Berfuche had been relieved and two fresh policemen kept inquisitive onlookers at bay. They saluted me. I could see roaches slipping between the weeds in the water. From time to time one of them would come up to the surface to test the air, then it would go back down, flicking its tail as it rejoined the group. Droplets twinkled in the grass. Everything had changed already. The imprint of Belle de jour's body on the bank was no longer there. There was not a trace. Two ducks were fighting over a cushion of watercress. In the end one of them pinched the other's neck, and it flew off scattering plaintive cries in its wake.

I hung about for a while, thinking about nothing in particular, or perhaps of Clémence and the little one in her tummy. I felt quite ashamed, I remember now, to be thinking about them, about our happiness, so close to the spot where a little girl had been killed. I knew that I would see them again in a few hours: her and her tummy. It was as round as a prize pumpkin that tummy. When I put my ear up to it I could hear the child paddling about and sense its sleepy movements. I was probably the happiest man in the world that freezing cold day. Close by, men were killing and dying as a matter of course, and a faceless assassin had strangled a little ten-year-old lamb. Yes, I was the happiest of men, and I couldn't even feel guilty about it.

The strange thing about the enquiry was that it was entrusted to nobody and to everybody at the same time. Mierck made quite a meal of it. The mayor poked his nose in too. The police sniffed at it from a safe distance. On top of all that, there was a colonel who sort of took charge of manoeuvres. He turned up the morning after the crime, claiming that, because we were in a state of war and so close to the front, he would be giving the orders. His name was Matziev, which had a Russian ring to it, but he looked like a Neapolitan dancer, with a voice as smooth as pomade, glossy hair slicked back over his head, a thin moustache. He carried himself well on supple legs and had the body of a Greek wrestler. In other words, he was an Adonis in uniform.

We knew straight away the sort of man we were dealing with: someone who saw blood and death as a hobby, but who kept on the right side, the side where blood could flow without offence. The only hotel in town had given up and closed its doors, so he took lodgings with Bassepin, who let out a few rooms and sold coal, oil, cooking fat and tins of bully beef to the soldiers that passed through.

They were the best years of Bassepin's life, the war years! Travelling kilometres to buy things at a pittance and then selling them on for a fortune. Lining his pockets very handsomely, working day and night, showering the quartermasters with everything they needed and several things they didn't and sometimes – when a regiment was leaving town – taking back what he had sold to them only to flog it on to the next lot that came in, and so on. The business makes the man, and he made the most of it.

The period just after the war was not bad for him either. He cashed in on the rush to honour the fallen heroes, expanding into the commemoration business, selling cast-iron soldiers and French fighting cocks by the tonne. Every mayor in the Eastern region had to have one of his soldiers (flags high, rifles at the ready) which were designed for him by a consumptive painter, an 'exhibition medal-holder'. He had them in all prices to suit all budgets, twenty-three different designs in the catalogue, with optional extras like marble plinths, gold lettering, obelisks, little children in zinc handing wreaths to the conquerors, and young goddesses baring consoling bosoms in an allegorical manner. Bassepin did a good trade in remembrance. Town councils settled their debts with the dead and dying in a very visible and lasting way, monuments surrounded by gravel and lime trees, round which every

11 November an eager brass band would play rousing songs of triumph and insipid laments. By night, dogs lifted their legs and pigeons shat their own commemorations.

Bassepin had a big pot-belly, a moleskin hat which he never took off summer or winter, and a mouthful of liquorice and black teeth. At fifty, he had never been known to have a romantic adventure. He kept what money he had, not drinking it, not gambling with it, and never chucking it away in the brothels of V. He had no vices. No little luxuries. No longings. Just an obsession for buying and selling, amassing gold for no reason, unless it was for the sake of it. Rather like those people who stack their barns full of hay but have no livestock. Why shouldn't he? He died as rich as Croesus, in '31, of septicaemia. It is incredible what a tiny little wound can do, rot your life, even cut it short. It started with his foot, a little graze, hardly breaking the skin. Five days later he was stiff as a board, and blue, covered in blotches from head to foot. He looked like an African savage daubed in war paint, but without the frizzy hair or the spear. There was no one to mourn him or shed a tear. It was not that he was hated – far from it – but a man who was only interested in gold and who never looked at anyone did not deserve to be pitied. He'd got what he wanted, and few can say as much. Perhaps that was his purpose on this earth, collecting all those coins. It's no more stupid than any other. He certainly made the most of it. After his death all his money went to the State: what a lovely widow the state makes, always happy and never in mourning.

When Matziev moved in, Bassepin gave him the best rooms and raised his moleskin hat every time he saw him, so that everyone could see, between a handful of struggling hairs on his turnip-coloured scalp, a large strawberry birthmark that looked just like the continent of America.

The first important thing that Matziev did when he arrived

in our little town was to order a phonograph. He could be seen at his open bedroom window for hours on end, despite the relentless cold, smoking cigars as thin as shoelaces, and rewinding his crackling machine every five minutes. He listened to the same song over and over again, a repetitive little number which had been fashionable a few years before, in a time when we all still thought that the world would go on for ever and that you only had to convince yourself you were happy to be happy:

> Caroline, put on your little patent shoes . . .
> Caroline, let me tell you . . .

Twenty times a day, one hundred times a day, Caroline put on her adorable shoes and all the while the Colonel smoked, wrist elegantly limp, rings on every finger. He smoked those stinking little brown things and his black eyes wandered over the rooftops. I still have that song in my head to this day: it makes me grind my teeth. When we heard it back then, we were all still thinking of Belle de jour, and trying to imagine the face of the monster who had done that to her. That song of the Colonel's drilled a nice neat little hole in our heads. When all was said and done, that song was first cousin to the Judge's eggs, those 'little worlds' enjoyed so close to the body. It's hardly surprising that Mierck and Matziev, though they had never met before and were like chalk and cheese, got on so well together, like pigs in shit. When it comes down to it, it's just a question of the kind of muck, that's all.

xiii

But nothing is simple. Only saints and angels are never wrong. Given what I am about to tell you, and given what he did, you'd probably put Matziev up there with the real bastards. They're the most abundant species on earth, after all, and they breed like cockroaches.

And yet this man, twenty-three years before the *Affaire*, had trampled all over his own career, had consigned himself to the rank of lieutenant for years while others claimed their stripes, all because he supported Dreyfus and, mark my words, he didn't just support him in theory as so many did! No, Matziev had real balls. He stood up for the little captain very publicly, proclaimed his innocence, challenging his fellow officers, with that one move turning against him everyone and anyone who could have helped him to a nice promotion. Who could have shot him up towards the stars, those gold stars soldiers sew on their shoulders.

That's History, with a capital H as they say, but it gets forgotten, lost in an attic, among old piles of rubbish.

When my father died in '26, I had to go back to the crooked old house where I was born and grew up. I didn't want to spend longer there than necessary. That house and I had already had our fair share of deaths. My mother, God rest her, had died when I was only little. And now it was my father. The house of my childhood had something of the grave about it now.

Even the village was nothing like the village I had known. Everyone had moved out after the war. After four years of bombardment they had abandoned the gutted houses and the potholed roads. Only two of the villagers had stayed: my father and Fantin Marcoire, a wizened old boy who talked to the fish in the river. To my father, leaving would have meant that the Boches had won after all. Fantin Marcoire lived with a very old cow which he called Madame, and which slept by his side in the cowshed. They ended up very alike, the smell and everything, except that the cow probably had a bit more common sense than Fantin Marcoire and harboured a bit less anger. Fantin loathed my father. And my father gave back as good as he got. Two madmen in a ghost village, hurling abuse at each other over the ruins, even throwing stones at each other like wrinkled children. Every morning before the sun was up Fantin Marcoire came and pulled his trousers down to shit outside my father's door. And every evening my father would wait until Fantin Marcoire had gone to his bed by his cow's flank before going and doing the same outside *his* door.

This went on for years, and became almost a ritual. A courtesy in bowel movements. They had known each other since their schooldays. They had hated each other without really knowing why ever since. They had chased the same girls, played the same games, knew the same sorrows and pain. And time had left its mark on them as it does on all of us.

'So he's dead then?'

'Good and dead, Monsieur Marcoire.'

'The bastard, how could he do it to me!'

'He'd got to that age.'

'Does that mean I have too?'

'It does.'

'The shit, doing that to me! What am I going to do now?'

'You could move out, go somewhere else, Monsieur Mar-coire.'

'It's a great idea, you little brat, go somewhere else . . . You're as stupid as your father! The bastard! What was he here for but to bugger my life up . . . What's going to happen to me . . . ? Do you think he suffered?'

'I don't think so.'

'Not even a little?'

'Maybe, I don't know, how can you tell?'

'Oh, I'll suffer, that's for sure, I can feel it starting already. Bastard . . .'

Fantin set off along what had been the main street of the village, detouring round the old potholes. He looked like a ballerina, a ballerina right at the end of her career, filled with rage, stopping every few metres to call my father a 'waster' and an 'idiot'. Then he disappeared around the corner of Camille's shop – *Favours, trinkets and novelties* – the slats of its broken shutters like the keys of a ruined piano.

My father's house was like the den of a wild animal. I tried hard to remember the tunes I had known, images from my childhood. But there was nothing there any more. A layer of dirt and dust dulled every surface. It was like a tomb for some mis-anthrope who wanted to take everything with him but, in the end, could not. I remembered what we had been told at school about the pharaohs and their tombs filled to the gunwales with all their worldly goods. That was what it was like, my father's house, except that he was no pharaoh. And instead of gold and precious stones, there was just dirty crockery and empty wine bottles, in every room of the house, piled in great, tumbling heaps.

I had never loved my father, and I didn't even know why not. And I had never hated him either. We just never talked.

My mother's death was always there between us, a silent wall neither of us dared break through.

He had set up camp in what had once been my room, built a stronghold of rubbish and piles of old newspapers which tottered to the ceiling. All that was left of the window was a fine arrow slit through which he could see the dilapidated building in which Fantin Marcoire lived. On the floor near this open-ing there were two catapults made of hazel wood and rubber tubing, the sort of thing youngsters use to fire stones at crows, or a policeman's backside. Beside them lay a supply of rusted staples and bent screws, a piece of half-eaten *saucisson*, a litre of heavy wine, and a dirty glass.

That was where my father had carried on his war, bombarding his enemy every time he came out of his house. I could see him there, drinking and ruminating for hours, keeping one eye on the strip of daylight, listening out for sounds in the street, filling up his glass as a way of cheating time as he checked his watch. And then suddenly, he'd pick up a catapult, fill it with shot, aim at the other man, wait to hear his yell, see him rubbing his thigh or his cheek or his backside, maybe there would be some blood; listening out for the cursing and then slapping his thighs and laughing till he choked, laughing until the laughter disintegrated into grotesque hiccups, no longer laughing, but mumbling, catching his breath; boredom, sadness, emptiness catching up with him. Then more wine, drinking, drinking it down in one, hand shaking. Wondering what he added up to: not much at all. Wondering how long this could go on: a day was a very long time, and he would have to hold on a bit longer, and there would be more days, more and more days, drinking straight out of the bottle, and thinking that he was worthless.

As I left the room my shoulder knocked over a pile of newspapers, which collapsed like autumn leaves. The past

[76]

slithered down, lost days, distant dramas. And in among it was that name: Matziev. In huge letters. It had happened in the December of 1894, but let me read it as it was written: *'Lieutenant Isidore Matziev,'* the article began, *'in full uniform, before a meeting gathered in the back room of a café, proclaimed his belief in Captain Dreyfus's innocence. He was met with applause from his audience of trade unionists and revolutionaries, and he also claimed that he was ashamed to belong to an army which locked up the righteous and left true traitors to run free.'* The article went on to say that the crowd gave him an ovation, which was interrupted only by the arrival of the police who made a number of arrests, including Matziev's, and dished out a good many blows with their truncheons. Considered a *'troublemaker for breaking the code of silence and sullying the French army's honour with his words, Lieutenant Matziev appeared the following day before a military tribunal which condemned him to six months' close arrest.'*

The author of the article, not the most inspired of journalists, concluded by saying he was scandalised by the attitude of this young soldier whose name, incidentally 'had a strong whiff of the Jewish or the Russian, possibly both'. He had signed himself Amédée Prurion. A stupid name for a stupid bastard. What happened to him, I wondered. Did he go on spewing out this mundane trash which must have ended up wiping bottoms in a good many houses? Prurion. His name sounded like a disease, an old sore that never heals. I'm sure he had a face like a cockroach, this Prurion, and bandy legs, stinking breath, everything that goes with the kind of folk who insist on spitting out their bile and then go and get joylessly pickled in empty bars, squinting at the haunches of the overworked waitress as she mops the floor and sprinkles it with sawdust. If this Prurion is dead now, then that's one shit less on this earth. If he's alive, then he must be a sorry sight by now. Hatred is a cruel marinade: it flavours the meat with failure. Even though I knew Matziev when he had become a bastard, there was no denying that he was a better man than this one. Once in his life at least, he did himself honour. How many of us can say as much?

I kept the article, as proof. Of what exactly? And I left the house and never went back. Life does not allow any going back. I thought of Matziev, with his pencil moustache, his twisted cigars and his phonograph spouting out that little song. He got lost too, with all his kit, once the *Affaire* was settled – as far as they were concerned, of course. He probably peddled all about the place with his *Caroline*, looking for nothing in particular. When you looked him in the eye, his expression seemed to say that he had arrived. But where had he arrived? No one knew. He had arrived all the same. And it was all over, there was no point getting worked up about anything. It was over. All he had to do was wait for his final appointment.

It snowed for hours that night. I could hear it as I tried to get to sleep. Actually, what I heard was silence. I sensed the whiteness through the half-closed shutters, and knew that it was gathering strength by the hour, like an invasion.

All that, the silence and the carpet of white, cuts me off from the world even more. As if I needed it. Clémence loved the snow. She would say: 'If the snow comes, how beautiful our little one will look in it.' She did not know how right she was. It clothed her in beauty too.

At seven o'clock I pushed the door open. The countryside looked fresh from the pâtisserie: cream and clouds of sugar everywhere. I blinked. It was like a miracle. The low sky rolled its lumpy weight over the crest of the hill, and the factory, that roaring one-eyed monster, now purred gently. The world seemed new. The first morning of a new world. It was like being the first man. Before our misdeeds turned it to slush. I am not sure how to say this. It's not easy to find the words, and I was never much of a talker in my life. I say 'in my life' as if I were dead. And deep down I am. I truly am. I have been dead for a long time. I pretend that I am alive, but my sentence has been deferred, that's all.

My every step betrays my trust with its sly, rheumatic pain, but still I am led round in circles, like a donkey tied to a mill-stone, grinding spoiled grain. I must come back now to the heart of the matter. It was thanks to those treacherous foot-steps that I found myself back on the banks of the little canal, a fine thread of green edged with melting stars in the surrounding whiteness. My feet sank into the snow, and I thought of the Berezina River. Perhaps that was what I needed, an epic, to persuade me that life does actually have a meaning, that though I am losing myself I am at least heading in the right direction, walking straight into the history books, for centuries to come. And that I was right all those times I put off the end, taking Gachentard's gun out of my mouth at the last minute. There were mornings when I felt as empty as a dry well . . . and the taste of the shotgun; your tongue sticks to it, it stings, smells of wine and rock.

Some stone martens had been fighting, and had left crazy curling words inscribed all over the blanket of snow. Their tummies had written little trails that peeled away, criss-crossed and ploughed into each other only to part again before stop-ping quite suddenly, as if the game was over, the two of them taking off in the blinking of an eye.

'Stupid as ever.'

I thought the cold was playing tricks on me.

'Do you want to catch your death?' the voice went on. It sounded as if it came from far away, all rasping and clanking like a chest full of medals. No need to turn round to know who was talking. Joséphine Maulpas. Same age as me and from the same village. Arrived here when she was thirteen years old to work as a maid, which she did until she was twenty, going from one wealthy family to another, and dipping a little deeper into the bottle every time until she eventually fell right in and couldn't get a job anywhere. Shown the door by everyone, thrown out, turned down, seen off, washed up. Till the only trade left to her was in skin: rabbits, moles, weasels, ferrets, foxes, every kind of stinking skin, all still dripping with blood, freshly flayed by Joséphine's penknife. Thirty years or more she spent traipsing the streets with her goitrous barrow: 'Rabbit skins! Animal skins! Rabbit skins!', she'd call out, till she too smelled of dead meat, till her face took on the look of a slain animal, that violet colour, dull-eyed . . . and to think she had once been pretty as a picture.

Joséphine (the children called her Skin) would sell these treasures of hers on for a pittance to Elphège Crochemort, who tanned them in a former mill on the banks of the Guerlante, six kilometres upstream from town. The old mill was more or less in ruins, and water gushed through it like a holed boat, but still it stood, season after season.

Crochemort rarely came into town. When he did, you knew it by the smell. You could easily tell which street he had taken because of the terrible stench which hung over him summer and winter, morning and night, as if he had marinated himself for days on end in his own vats of alkali. He was a tall, good-looking man with glossy black hair swept back over his head, and twinkling azure-blue eyes. Very good-looking, and single. I always saw him as one of those people in the Greek stories, having to roll stones or have their livers eaten for all eternity. Perhaps Crochemort really had committed some crime, some dark and inescapable sin, and this was how he paid for it, all alone and smelling of dead meat. Rub him down with lavender and jasmine and the women would have been falling at his feet.

Joséphine brought her haul to him every week. The smell didn't bother her. And she had turned her back on men long ago and kept out of their way now, having only been married to herself in all her life. Elphège Crochemort used to welcome her like a queen, she told me, with a glass of fortified wine, and some charming words about the rain, the skins, the fine weather to come, smiling that smile of his. Then he'd pay her, help her unload the barrow and, finally, would walk back to the path with her as if he were courting her.

For twenty years, Joséphine had been living at the very end of the rue des Chablis, practically out in the fields. It wasn't a house, just a few planks blackened by the rain and held together by an everyday miracle. A little cabin as dark as a coal shed, fit to scare the children. People thought it must be filled to the stinking gunwales with pelts, corpses, mutilated birds, mice nailed to boards. No one ever visited.

Except that I did. Twice. It was beyond belief. It was like going through the gates of the underworld and stepping into a realm of light: like a dolls' house, clean as a new pin, all pinks and little curly ribbons tied all over the place.

'You'd rather I lived in filth?' Joséphine said, the first time as I stood there gaping like a bream out of water, eyes everywhere. There was a vase of irises on a beautifully covered table, framed pictures of saints and cherubs on the walls, the kind of things that priests give to communicants and altar boys.

'Do you believe?' I asked Joséphine, indicating the glowing gallery. She shrugged her shoulders, not mocking me but rather to show me how pitiful the question was.

'If I had beautiful copper pans I'd hang them up and the effect would be the same. It makes you feel the world isn't so ugly, that every now and then there's a little flash of gold. That's what life boils down to, looking for those scraps of gold.'

I felt a hand on my shoulder. Then another hand, and finally a warm woollen sleeve.

'Why've you come back, Dadais?' That was her nickname for me, ever since we were seven years old, but I never knew why. I was about to reply, was looking around for some fine words, down there in the snow by the water, in my shirtsleeves. But my lips trembled and I suddenly felt that I could not move at all any more.

'Well, you've come back, haven't you?'

'I was passing. It's not the same. I don't have anything to be sorry for. I did what I had to do. I did my bit, and you know it.'

'I believed you!'

'You were the only one who did, then . . .'

Joséphine rubbed my shoulders. She shook me, and the blood whipped back into my veins. Then she took me by the arm and we left. We made an odd couple, in the snow of that winter's morning, walking along without speaking to each other. Sometimes I tried to find the little girl's features in her old face. But I might as well have tried to find flesh on a skeleton. I gave in like a child. I could have closed my eyes and slept on my feet, still putting one foot in front of the other, hoping deep down never to open my eyes again, the walk of a dead man, or just some pointless, endless slow promenade.

Once back at my house, Joséphine took it upon herself to sit me down in the big armchair, swaddling me in three thick layers of wool as if I was a tiny baby again. She disappeared into the kitchen. I lifted my feet up to the stove and gradually every part of my body came back to life, the strength, as well as the pain, the creaking and the chapping. She handed me a scalding hot bowl which smelled of plums and lemon. I drank without a word. She drank too. She finished her bowlful and clicked her tongue:

'Why did you never remarry?'

'What about you? Why did you never marry?'

'I knew everything there was to know about men before I was fifteen. You don't know what it's like being a servant! Never again, I said to myself, and I stuck to it. It wasn't the same with you . . .'

'I talk to her every day, you know. There was never room for anyone else.'

'You wanted to be like the Prosecutor, admit it!'

'It was nothing like that.'

'That's what you say . . . All this time you've been mulling it over – you're as good as married to him. You've even grown to look like each other, like an old married couple.'

'Don't be stupid, Fifine.'

We sat in silence for a while, then she went on: 'I saw him that terrible night, I swear I did. I saw him with my own eyes, even if the fool didn't believe me – what was his name again, that pig in a coat?'

'Mierck.'

'What a name! Dead, I hope?'

'In '31. Horse kicked his head in.'

'All the better – I like it when some people go. But you were in charge of the case, why didn't he believe *you*?'

'He was the judge . . .'

I climbed back down through the years again and there it was, where I left it. I know the way so well. It's like going home.

Joséphine had come looking for me three days after Belle's body was found. The investigation was going round in circles. The police were interrogating people left, right and centre. Matziev was listening to that song. Mierck had gone back to V, and I was trying to make sense of it all.

Clémence opened the door to her, laughing, hands round that great tummy of hers. She was always laughing. She knew Joséphine a little and was happy to let her in, despite her strange appearance and her reputation as a witch.

'She was so gentle, your wife . . .' Joséphine handed me another full bowl. 'I don't remember her face very well,' she added, 'but I remember she was kind, that everything about her was kind, the way she spoke, the way she looked.'

'I don't remember either,' I said, 'I can't see her face . . . I try to so often, can feel it coming towards me, then it dissolves, and there's nothing left, and I thump myself, yell at myself . . .'

'Why do you do that, fool?'

'Forgetting the face of the woman I loved – what a bastard.'

Joséphine shrugged her shoulders:

'Bastards, saints . . . I've never met one or the other. Nothing's black or white. And it's the same with souls. You're a grey soul, like the rest of us.'

'Those are just words.'

'Have words ever hurt you?'

I had asked her to sit down and she had told me her story, spilled it all out in very precise terms. Clémence had gone up to our bedroom and I knew what she was doing: needles, balls of blue and pink wool, lace – it had been going on for weeks already. While Joséphine was talking, I thought of Clémence in that room so close by, fingers sliding along the needles, tiny elbows and feet pushing and kicking in her tummy.

Then, little by little, into that room came someone else: Belle de jour, soaking wet, sat down beside me, and it was as if she had come to listen, to agree or disagree with what Joséphine had to say. Little by little, I stopped thinking about anything else. I listened, and I looked at Belle de jour, her dead face, her young dead face, running with water, eyes closed, lips blue from the last cold blast. From time to time, I thought she was smiling. She would tilt her head, her mouth seeming to say: 'Yes, that's true, that's right. It was just as she says. That's what happened.'

So, the day before the body was found. Towards six o'clock. Dusk, a time of daggers and stolen kisses. Joséphine is pulling her barrow and heading for home, drawing warmth from the flask of brandy she always keeps in the pocket of her smock. Oddly enough, despite the cold, the streets are filling up with the halt and the lame out for the day: they're all there, the amputees, the legless, the mutilated, the blind, the trepanned and the half-crazy, trailing from one bar to another, emptying glasses to fill their hearts.

In the beginning, after the first fighting, it felt very strange seeing these fellows coming through with their faces re-arranged by exploding shells and their bodies carved up by machine-gun fire, while we, the same age as them, kept nice and warm and quietly got on with our little lives.

Of course we knew the war was going on. We saw the mobilisation notices and we read about it in the papers. But, deep down, it was all a pretence. We'd found a way out of it. We coped with it as if it was a dream, a bitter memory. It wasn't us, it didn't touch our lives.

So, when the first convoy of casualties arrived – and I mean casualties, men on flea-ridden stretchers, with red pulp instead of flesh, groaning softly in the backs of lorries, calling dismally, reverently, for their mothers or their wives – when it arrived in our town, then it hit us. Suddenly, everyone went very quiet, and we all came out to look at them, these shadows of men, being carried through to the clinic. There were two rows of them, two thick rows, a guard of honour, a guard of horror . . . The women bit their lips and wept and wept, and the rest of us felt stupid and useless deep down, and ashamed, and it is not pretty to say this but it has to be said: we also felt glad, brutally, unhealthily happy, that it was them and not us lying there.

That was in September 1914. The first casualties were spoiled rotten. Visits from one end of the day to the next, bottles, pies, cakes, liqueurs, fine cambric shirts, corduroy trousers, ham, good wine.

Then time did its work. Time, and the sheer quantity of injured. More came every day, great batches of them. We grew accustomed to them. We even became fed up with them. Disgusted. They resented us for being spared, and we resented them for rubbing our noses in it, their bandages and missing limbs, their cracked skulls, their crooked mouths and blasted noses, all the things we were so happy not to have.

Then it was as if there were two towns: ours and theirs. Two towns sharing the same space, turning their backs on each other, drinking at different cafés, walking on different streets, keeping different hours. Two worlds. There were insults, rows, fights. The Blachart widow was about the only go-between, opening her thighs to both camps, civilians or soldiers, day or night, whoever they were. The queue outside her house, which sometimes stretched a good ten metres, was neutral ground. Men spoke to each other, forgot and fraternised as they waited for the oblivion lying hidden in the widow's belly. She spent the whole day, or very nearly, with her legs spread apart on her double bed, with the portrait of her dead husband all done up in his wedding suit smiling over her from beneath a sash of black crêpe. And every ten minutes another urgent young man came to take the deceased's place, which had been surrendered three years earlier when a tonne of coal crashed down on his head at the factory.

Plenty of old hags spat at the Blachart widow behind her back in the street. Names were bandied about too: 'Whore, tart, slut, bitch, slag, hussy, hooker,' and plenty more. Agathe – that was her name – could not have cared less. There were people who were given medals for doing less for the war effort than she did. You have to be fair. Giving your body and a bit of warmth, even if it is for the sake of a few coins . . . How many of us do that?

In '23 Agathe Blachart closed up shop, packed a small suitcase, said goodbye to no one, and left for V on the mail coach. From there she took the express train to Châlons. In Châlons she changed onto the Paris train. Three days later she was in Le Havre where she set sail on board *Boréal*. Two months later she stepped ashore in Australia.

The books say that Australia is all deserts, kangaroos, wild dogs, endless expanses of flat land inhabited by cavemen, and towns as new as freshly minted coins. I am not really sure we should believe them. Books sometimes lie. I do know, though, that Australia has had the Blachart widow since 1923. Maybe she remarried. Maybe she even has children, a business.

Maybe everyone smiles at her and says good morning in a respectful way. Maybe, by putting oceans between herself and us, she managed to forget us altogether, and was washed clean, no past, no pain, nothing. Maybe.

None of which alters the fact that on that blessed evening the injured were not all at her house. They were milling around the streets – the place was overflowing with them, most of them blind drunk and making nuisances of themselves, shouting and vomiting, great gangs of them hanging around together. So, to avoid them, Joséphine and her barrow take another route home. Rather than going down the rue du Pressoir, she carries on along the rue des Mesiaux, down the side of the church, up behind the *mairie* and over towards the cemetery. She feels happier going along the little canal, even if it is narrow, even if it will be difficult with her loaded barrow. Even though the detour adds a good kilometre to her journey.

It's cold. Everything is crackling with frost. Joséphine's nose is running and her flask is empty. The first star is pinned to the blue-grey sky like a silver nail. Snow crunches beneath the barrow, the pelts are stiff as boards. Joséphine lifts a hand to wipe away an icicle from her nose. And it is then that she sees Belle de jour in the distance, about sixty metres away admittedly, motionless by the edge of the little canal, deep in conversation with a tall man who leans towards her, as if he wants to see or hear her more clearly. And this man, standing there stiffly, dressed all in black, on that winter's evening as the weary day prepared to bow out, this man was the Prosecutor, Pierre-Ange Destinat himself. Swear to God, cross my heart and hope to die. It was him. With her, the girl, in the gathering darkness. Just the two of them alone together.

Joséphine was glued to the spot by the twilit scene and could not go on. Why? Can't say. If you had to explain everything you do, every little sign or thought, every move, you'd never get to the end of it. So there was Joséphine, stopped short, not so odd really, on that mid-December Sunday evening, transfixed like a dog by the sight of the Prosecutor from V deep in conversation with a little flower, putting his hand on her shoulder, yes, his hand on her shoulder. She swore to that too. 'At sixty metres, in the dark, you saw a hand on a shoulder, and you were blind drunk! You're joking!' That's what they said when they plagued her about it later. But I will come back to that. Joséphine stood by what she said. It was him. It was her. And it would take more than five sips of brandy for her to start seeing things!

Well, so what? Destinat talking to the child, what was wrong with that? He knew her. She knew him. Seeing them together, on the actual spot where she would be found strangled the next day – what did it prove? Nothing. Nothing. Or everything?

There was no sound from the bedroom now. Perhaps Clémence had fallen asleep. And the little one too. Joséphine had finished her story and was looking at me. I could see it all as she described it. Belle de jour had left the room, sodden clothes clinging to her slender, frozen body. She had smiled at me and gone.

'Then?' I ask Joséphine.
  'Then what?'
  'Did you go up to them?'
  'I'm not stupid. I'd rather keep the Prosecutor at a distance!'
  'So?'
  'So, I turned around.'
  'You left them like that?'
  'What do you expect me to do? Go and hold a lantern for them? Warm their feet?'
  'And the girl, you're sure it was her?'

[90]

'Come on, how many girls do you see in the street with a golden yellow hood like that? I'd seen her going into her aunt's house earlier in the day wearing it. It was definitely her, you can be sure of it.'

'What would she have been doing down by the canal?'

'What I was doing, for God's sake! Keeping out the way of drunken soldiers! Another two hundred metres and she'd have been back on the square catching the six o'clock mail coach . . . Got anything to drink, by the way? This talking is making me thirsty.'

I took out two glasses, a bottle, some cheese, a sausage and an onion. We drank and ate in silence, without exchanging another word. I looked over at Joséphine, wanting to see the picture through her eyes as she had described it to me. She nibbled her food like a mouse and drank great gulps with a supple, practised motion of her tongue. Outside the snow fell heavily. It blew against the windowpanes, spelling out words that melted away almost before they were formed, like tears on an absent cheek. Snow turned to slush. The frost was picking up its shredded rags and leaving. Tomorrow's face would be wet and smeared with mud – like a bit-part actress after the curtain falls on her one moment in the limelight.

It was late. I made up a kind of bed in a corner of the kitchen. I had persuaded Joséphine to come with me to V at dawn to tell Mierck everything. She fell asleep in a great heap, and as she slept she spoke a few words which I could not quite catch. A cannon boomed from time to time, but listlessly, just to remind us it was there, like a bell ringing out bad news.

I did not venture into the bedroom. I was afraid I would make a noise and wake Clémence. Instead I settled myself into an armchair. I still have that chair, it folds around me gently like a huge sheltering hand. I sat thinking of everything Joséphine had said. Then my eyes closed.

We left at dawn. Clémence was up, and had made a scalding pot of coffee and had wrapped a litre bottle of *vin chaud* for us to take. She waved to us both from the doorstep, and smiled at me, at me alone. I took a step towards her, I so wanted to kiss her, but I did not dare in front of Joséphine. So I waved back. And that was that.

Since then, not one day has gone by when I have not regretted that kiss I failed to give her.

'Safe journey,' she said. Those were her last words. They are still there, in my ears, intact, and I play them every evening, my little treasures. Safe journey . . . I no longer have her face, but I swear I have her voice.

It took us four hours to get to V. Every furrow was filled with water and the horse kept getting bogged down in the sludge. The snow was melting fast, and the road surface disappeared beneath the torrents that streamed into the ditches. And then we would have to huddle by the side of the road to let the troop convoys get past, on foot, in carts and lorries, on their way to the front. Young soldiers looked silently at us with melancholy eyes, like docile animals in blue, allowing themselves to be led to the great abattoir.

Crusty, Judge Mierck's clerk, sat us down in an anteroom and left us. I knew that room with its red silk hangings well. I had already had plenty of opportunities to sit there ruminating about the human condition, about boredom, the weight of an hour, a minute, even a second. I could have closed my eyes and drawn on a piece of paper the position of every piece of furniture and every object, the number of petals on each dried anemone sighing in the stoneware vase on the mantelpiece. Joséphine snoozed with her hands on her thighs. From time to time her head dropped and she would sit back up sharply, as if she had been jabbed with a cattle prod.

At last, after an hour, Crusty came back to get us, scratching his cheek a little. Shreds of dead skin fell onto his black suit with its shiny elbows and knees. Without a word he led us into the judge's office.

At first we could see nothing, but we could hear two people laughing. One had a hawking laugh, thick and throaty, and I recognised it. The other was new to me, but I very soon came to recognise it. A bank of pungent smoke hung about the room, separating the two of us from the fat judge at his desk and his companion. We weren't sure what to do. Our eyes gradually became accustomed to the fog, and the judge's face emerged, along with that of the other man. It was Matziev. The two of them laughed on, the one in uniform drawing on his cigar, the judge hugging his belly, as if we did not exist, as if we were not standing there just a few paces from them. Then they slowly, unhurriedly, let their laughter die down. There was a silence that lasted too long, and it was only then that Mierck laid his big green fish eyes on us. The officer smoked and smiled, looking at us as if we were closely related to worms.

'Right then. What is it?' the judge said with a note of irritation, staring at Joséphine as if she were an animal.

Mierck did not like me and I did not like him. Our jobs meant we had to meet frequently, but we never exchanged a word more than we had to. Our conversations were brief, cold, conducted without eye contact. I made the introductions and, before I even had a chance to summarise what Joséphine had told me, Mierck cut me off, addressing himself directly to her.

'Occupation?'

Joséphine opened her mouth wide, searching for words, but she was too slow and the judge became impatient.

'Is she stupid or deaf or what? Occupation!'

Joséphine cleared her throat, glanced over at me and eventually managed: 'Salvage . . .'

The judge looked at the soldier and they exchanged a smile, then Mierck went on: 'And what does she salvage?'

This was the judge's way of reducing a person to nothing. He didn't say *you*, but *he* or *she*, as if you were not there, as if you were invisible. It was assault by pronoun. As I said before, he knew how to use language.

I saw Joséphine's face burn red, and a murderous light gleamed in her eye. If she had had a gun or a knife in her hand, Mierck would have been waving this world goodbye right away. We do a lot of mental and verbal killing every day, although we don't realise it. Actual killings, on the other hand, are few and far between if you think about it. It is really only in wartime that any balance is established between our desires and reality.

Joséphine took a deep breath and began to describe, in good, clear terms, the tough trade of which she had no reason to be ashamed.

Mierck dug at her again: 'Look what we've got here! She lives off corpses, is that what she's saying?' and he laughed the false laugh of the fool he was, and Matziev – still sucking his cigar as if the world depended on it – joined him.

I put my hand on Joséphine's, and I started to talk. I explained, very simply and in detail, what she had told me the night before. Mierck, serious again, listened to me without interruption and when I had finished he turned to the officer. They exchanged an indecipherable look, then the judge picked up his paperknife in his right hand and twirled it around his blotter for a while. He made it dance, something between a polka and a quadrille, with all the urgency of a galloping stallion, and then he stopped just as quickly as he had started. And that was when Joséphine's torment began.

The judge and the officer opted for a joint offensive, although without actual consultation. When you are sliced from the same meat you don't need a discussion to understand each

[95]

other. Joséphine rode out their onslaught as best she could, standing by her version and occasionally looking over at me, her eyes saying: 'Why did I listen to you, why are we here, and when are these bastards going to leave me in peace?' I could do nothing to help her. I watched as they undermined her, and when Joséphine quite innocently admitted that she had warmed herself up that night with a few sips from her brandy flask, Mierck and Matziev tore her brutally to pieces with a slow succession of snide remarks. When they had finished, she lowered her head, gave a long sigh and looked at her swollen calloused hands. She had aged twenty years in ten minutes.

At this point they took a short break, as if between rubbers. Matziev lit another cigar and paced about. Mierck pushed back his armchair and hooked his thumbs into the pockets of his over-stretched waistcoat. I did not know what to do. I was about to speak when Mierck leapt to his feet.

'You're not needed any more! You can go. As for her,' and he looked over at Joséphine again, 'she will remain with us until we can establish the truth of what she has said.'

Joséphine turned towards me, terrified. I put my hand on her shoulder – sometimes we try to use a gesture when words cannot help any more – but the judge was already dragging me out to the anteroom where Crusty was dozing. He waved him away curtly, closed the door and came right up to me, so that our mouths almost touched, looking me full in the eye; then he spoke, very quietly, and I could see all the dead blood vessels on his face, the wrinkles, the bumps and the tiny warts, and I took his well-fed breath full in the face, a mingling of onions, fine wine, meat and bitter coffee.

'Nothing happened, do you hear me? That madwoman was dreaming . . . Seeing things, getting ideas, drunken ravings!

Nothing happened. And it goes without saying that I forbid you to trouble the Prosecutor with this. I forbid it! Besides, I have already told you, the enquiry is in the hands of Colonel Matziev now. You will take your orders from him. You may go.'

'And Joséphine Maulpas?' I managed to say.

'Three days in a cell will bring her round.'

He turned on his heel and went back to his office. And I stayed there, rooted to the spot like a bloody fool.

'Three days, I'll give you three days,' Joséphine went on. 'The pig kept me there for a week on stale bread and soup, dished up by a nun who was about as friendly as an axe handle . . . Shit! Are you sure he's pegged it?'

'Yes.'

'Thank God! Hell has its uses! I hope he saw it coming, and suffered for it . . . What about the other one, the shit with the cigar, is he dead?'

'I don't know. Maybe, maybe not.'

We stayed there like that for a long time, Joséphine and I, picking over the tangled scraps of our lives. As we talked over those long-ago events, we began to believe that not every card in the pack had been played, that we might still fit somewhere in the great mosaic of fate. And then, without knowing how, our conversation took us back to our childhood, to the smell of the meadows where we played blind man's buff, the fears we shared, the songs, water splashing in the fountains. The bells struck midday and brought us back to the present.

When Joséphine left she kissed me on both cheeks. She had never done that before. I liked those kisses. They put a seal on something. This ancient story, still raw and open, united us in a kinship of solitude. She turned the corner at the end of the street. I thought of Belle again.

The little thing used to come to our house every Sunday, and had done since she was eight years old. Eight then was not what it is today! By the time you were eight, you knew how to do everything, you had some common sense in you, and good strong arms. You were almost an adult.

Bourrache had a nose for money, as I have already said. He chose godparents for his girls by sniffing out the banknotes. That's why, when the girl was baptised, she found herself in the arms of a distant relation who lived in our town and who, by the time of the *Affaire*, was nearly eighty. Adélaïde Siffert was her name, a tall, knotty woman with a hand-carved face, hands like a butcher's and legs like a woodcutter's. An old maid and happy to be so, but with a good heart.

She had been a clerk at the *mairie* for forty years because she wielded a pen very prettily, making no mistakes or ink blotches. She had a small pension, which meant that she could live quite comfortably, frequently eating meat and drinking a glass of port every evening.

Every Sunday, then, Bourrache sent the girl to visit her godmother. She arrived on the midday coach and left by the six o'clock one. Adélaïde Siffert cooked roast pork, green beans (fresh when they were in season and bottled the rest of the year), salad and an apple pie. The menu never changed, she told me so herself. The girl had three helpings of pie. She told me that too. In the afternoon they'd do some sewing, and Belle de jour would help a little in the house. At five o'clock she would have another slice of pie and a cup of milky coffee, and then she would kiss her godmother, who would give her a banknote. The old woman would watch her leave. She had had her visit and the girl had her five francs, which Bourrache took from her as soon as she came home. Everyone was happy.

When the weather was bad, pouring with rain, or snowing heavily, the girl might stay the night with her godmother. No one worried, and she would catch the coach in the morning, the eight o'clock one.

On the evening of the murder – because according to Victor Desharet, who put his filthy hands into the child's body, opening up her belly as if he were unbuttoning a shirt, the crime was indeed committed that evening – Adélaïde had tried to hold the child back: it was already freezing solid and every breath you took hurt inside. But the little one wouldn't hear of it. 'I'm not cold at all, I'm lovely and warm in your hood!' she said, and that had flattered the old woman, because the hood in question, the golden-yellow one which you could spot from so far away, was something she had made for the child in panné velvet, lined with rabbit fur, and had given to her for her seventh birthday. Belle had tightened the ties, put on her mittens and breezed out, skipping into the distance, evaporating.

Grief kills. Very quickly. So does the feeling of being at fault, in anyone with a shred of morality. Adélaïde Siffert soon followed her goddaughter to the cemetery. Twenty-two days separated the two burials, not an hour more. In those three weeks the tears never stopped flowing down Adélaïde's cheeks, and I really mean they never stopped, not in the day (I can testify to that) or at night (I am prepared to swear to it). Good people go quickly. Everyone likes them, and death does too. Only bastards have tough skins. They usually die old, sometimes even in their beds. Happy as you please.

When I came out of Judge Mierck's office, I was feeling far from proud about having left Joséphine there. I wandered round V for a while with my hands in my pockets, getting my trousers dirty with all the mud.

The town seemed to be drunk. A whole batch of new recruits were stamping their feet to keep warm, laughing and swaggering around, all ready and eager, for the moment at least, to go and size up the Boches. The streets and bars had become uniformed zones, awash with new gaiters, flashy buttons and carefully sewn epaulettes. They were singing here, shouting there, whistling at the occasional girl who ventured into a shop. There was something wild and bloody about it all, like a giant rut, a surge of life in the raw; you could feel it bubbling up, ready to burst.

What was I doing amongst these poor uncomprehending fools? Most of them would make the return journey between four rough planks of larch, if they were lucky and some bits of them could be scraped off the floor of a shell crater or picked off the barbed wire.

I ploughed on like a blind man, and ended up at the door of Le Rébillon. At first I was shocked, then I realised that it was the only place I could go, that I had to go there. I had to push the door open and see Bourrache with his dark eyes and his tall frame, to shake his hand and mumble the stupid words we all use at times like that.

I had never seen that huge room empty before. Empty and silent. Not one table was laid. There was not one voice to be heard, not a clink of glass, not a wisp of smoke, not even the scent of cooking. There was only a meagre fire in the great hearth, and Bourrache sitting in front of it on a tiny stool, with his feet stretched out to the embers, his head bent on one side, looking into the abyss like a dying giant.

He did not hear me approach. I stood near him and said the words but he did not move, gave no reply. I saw the fire flicker, the last beautiful flames shrinking, writhing, struggling to stay alive and eventually dying down and disappearing. Then I saw that look of Clémence's, her eyes, her smile, her belly. I saw my own insolent happiness. And I saw Belle de jour's face, not dead and sodden, but as I had seen her the last time, alive and pink and vital as a stalk of green wheat, here in this very room, weaving between the tables with carafes of local wine for the customers.

The flames had given way to wisps of acrid grey smoke snaking out of the hearth and dancing about the room, bouncing off the brown ceiling. Then Bourrache moved, slowly, like an exhausted ox. He turned his face towards me. There was nothing in it, no expression. His great hands reached towards my neck and began to squeeze, to squeeze and squeeze, harder and harder and, strangely, I was not frightened. I let him do it. This was no murderer, not a madman either. This was a father who had just lost his child, whose sun was for ever eclipsed, his world dark. I was suffocating. Little pricks of white, little flashes danced before me, and I saw Bourrache's face, scarlet, trembling, and then suddenly he snapped his hands away from my neck, as if he had burned himself on a red-hot iron, and slumped weeping to the floor.

I caught my breath. I was covered in sweat. I helped Bourrache to a chair at the nearest table. He gave himself up, without any resistance. He sobbed and sniffed. I knew where the bottles of plum brandy and the glasses were kept and I poured two glasses to the brim. I helped him drink, then I knocked back my own, then another. Bourrache poured himself three, mechanically, downing them quickly one after the other. I saw him begin to focus, and he looked at me with a touch of surprise, as if wondering what I was doing there. Someone rapped on a pane very close by. An idiot of a soldier, beaming and peering in at the empty room, his nose against the window. Then he saw us and his smile dropped and he went away. I stayed for four hours. Four hours and two bottles of the strong stuff. Four hours and scarcely three words spoken. It was the least I could do.

And during that time, all alone, Clémence began to moan and writhe. And I wasn't with her. I didn't know.

As I came out of Le Rébillon, the icy rain knocked me into shape a little. The sky seemed to be bearing some grudge against humanity; bucketfuls of water were teeming down, splashing against the buildings. There was hardly anyone left on the streets. I hugged the walls as best I could, trying to shelter under my hands. I thought of Joséphine in her cell, cursing me, calling me every name under the sun. Thinking of it even made me smile a little.

By the time I reached the town tollpost, I was wringing wet. My feet were cold but my mind was clear, my head no longer spinning despite the brandy. The mail coach was there. There was a crowd around it, railing at a Captain in the Engineers who was trying to keep them all under control. I moved closer. Some of the men in the crowd started to shake their fists. The women were more resigned, waiting motionless as fenceposts, indifferent to the rain. That was when someone put their hand on my shoulder. It was the priest, Father Lurant.

'No chance of getting home – the roads have been requisitioned for the convoys. There are two regiments to get up to the front tonight. Look at them.'

I had not noticed them at first. But as soon as the priest pointed them out, they were all I could see: dozens, hundreds, perhaps more, waiting in complete silence, with their rifles on their shoulders and their kitbags on their backs, and they seemed to be surrounded by, and almost disappearing into, the darkness which was overtaking the day. They stood with absent eyes, not moving or speaking, apparently unaffected by the rain, an army of shadows. These same lads had been tramping all over V that day, jostling at the bars like cattle at a trough, bellowing and spewing, unbuttoning themselves in brothels, herds of them staggering about with bottles of wine in their hands. But they weren't laughing now. They were as stiff as statues, the same dark iron colour as well. Their eyes were not eyes but bottomless abysses, open onto nothing.

'Come on,' said the priest, 'there's no point staying here.' I followed him mechanically, while the officer still tried to appease the angry passengers who would not be getting home to their snug beds that evening.

It was not the first time they had requisitioned the road, which was in a pitiful state after three years' worth of lorries and the hooves of thousands of horses ploughing furrows through it. When they were preparing for an offensive, they reserved the road for troop convoys. All day and all night, without interruption, without pause, a trundling procession of pathetic ants headed slowly towards the shattered remains of their nest.

Father Lurant took me to the bishop's palace. The door was opened by a concierge with a yellow face and hair that looked like the pelt of a small animal. The priest explained the situation to him and, without a word, the concierge took us through a maze of corridors and stairways which smelled of wax and black soap, to a large bedroom in which two narrow iron beds stood in silent congress.

When I saw those little beds I thought of our bed at home, so big and deep. I would have liked to be beside Clémence, in her arms, seeking out the comfort I always found with her. I asked whether I could let her know I could not get home, which I usually did. I would ring the mayor and he would send his maid, Louisette, round to my house. But the concierge told me it was not worth trying. The telephone lines, like the roads, had been requisitioned, who knew for how long. This upset me, I remember. I would have liked Clémence to know, so that she did not worry. I would have liked her to know that I was thinking of her and of the child.

The priest undressed quite openly. He took off his cape, then his cassock, ending up in his vest and underpants in front of me, his stomach bulging forwards like a giant quince held in place by strip of flannel which he unwound. Then he laid his damp clothes out by the stove and went over to dry himself off and warm himself up. Seeing him like that, as good as naked, he seemed much younger, no older than me. It was like seeing him for the first time. He must have guessed what I was thinking. They're crafty these priests, they know how to get inside you. He looked at me and smiled. In the heat, his cape steamed like a locomotive, and mist rose from his cassock, which smelled of leaves and singed wool.

The concierge came back with two bowls of soup, a large loaf of brown bread, a piece of cheese as hard as wood, and a jug of wine. He left it all on a small table and bade us goodnight. I undressed and put my clothes close to the fire too. The same smells: wood, wool fat, smoke.

We ate seriously, too hungry for manners. Father Lurant had podgy, hairless hands, but the skin was delicate and the nails unchipped. He chewed every mouthful over and over and drank with his eyes closed. We left nothing, not a crumb or a crust. Our plates and the table itself were cleaned, our stomachs full. We talked for a long time, as we had never talked before. Of flowers mostly, about which he was passionate, 'the most beautiful proof, if any were needed, that there is a God,' he said. We talked about flowers there in that room, while around us it was dark and there was a war on. Somewhere out there was a killer who had strangled a child of ten. And at the same time, far from me, Clémence's blood was seeping into our bed, and she was crying out for help, and no one came.

I didn't know that you could talk about flowers. I mean, I didn't know that you could talk about men by talking about flowers, without using the words man, fate, death, end, loss. That's what I learned that night. The priest was also skilled with words, like Mierck, like Destinat. But he did beautiful things with them. He rolled them around with his tongue and his smile, and suddenly something insignificant would seem wonderful. They must teach them that at the seminary. How to capture the imagination with a few good words. He described his garden at the back of the presbytery, which no one ever saw because of the high wall around it. He told me about the anthemis, the hellebores, the petunias, the sweet williams, the pinks, the anemones, the sedums, the sweet alyssum, the ruffled peonies, the daturas, the flowers which live for only one season, and those that come back year after year. He spoke of those blooms that open in the evening and wilt by morning, and of those that glow, pink or violet, from dawn till dusk, velvet petals snapping shut once night falls as if a violent hand has strangled the life from them.

When he spoke of these last, the priest sounded different, no longer like a priest, or a gardener, but like a man full of pain and hurt. I held up my hand to stop him when he was about to say the name out loud in that dark room. I knew what that flower was called only too well, the name had been hammering in my head for two days, hammering and hammering. The girl's face came back to me, as if someone had slapped me. The priest fell silent. Outside, rain gave way to snow again, and snowflakes congregated in the window, like fireflies of ice, fleetingly ablaze with the illusion of light and life.

I tried for many years afterwards to get Belle de jour to bloom in our little garden, but I never succeeded. The seeds rotted stubbornly in the ground, would not leave the damp dark clod for the sky. Only couch grass and thistles prospered there, invading the whole garden, launching themselves to improbable heights, and drowning those few square metres with their deadly blooms. In the end I conceded defeat to them.

I often thought back to what the priest had said about flowers, God and proof. And I told myself that there were probably places in this world where God never set foot.

In '25, Father Lurant went off to evangelise the Annam tribes in the mountains of Indochina. He came to tell me he was going, I never really knew why. Perhaps because we two had once talked for hours in our underwear, sharing the same room and the same wine. I didn't ask him why he was leaving, going off like that as if he was still a young man. I just asked: 'What about your flowers?'

He looked at me and smiled with that same look in his eye, that priestly look I mentioned before, the one that goes right in and pulls out your soul like a two-pronged fork pulling out a snail. He said that where he was going there were thousands of flowers, and thousands that he did not know, had never seen, or only in books. He said that we cannot live life only in books, that there comes a time when we have to grasp it and all its beauty with our own two hands.

I thought of telling him how the opposite was true for me, that I had a bellyful of life every day and that if I could have found consolation in books I would have thrown myself into them. But when people are so far apart there is not much point talking. So I said nothing and we shook hands.

I can't say that I thought of him often in the years that followed, but I sometimes did. As well as a shotgun, my old colleague Edmond Gachentard had given me some pictures, and by pictures I don't mean images on paper but images that are created in your head, and stay there.

In his youth, Gachentard had been in the expeditionary force sent to Tonkin. He brought home a number of things, including a fever which made him go white as a leek and shake like a leaf; a green coffee pot which he preserved like a relic on the table in the dining room; a photograph of himself in uniform by some paddy-fields; and, most importantly, a kind of languid look, which overtook him when he thought of that part of the world, or spoke about it: the nights when tree frogs lulled you to sleep, the sticky heat, the great muddy river that dragged along trees and dead goats, water lilies and weeds. Sometimes Gachentard would even try to show me how the women danced there, the graceful hand movements, fingers bent, eyes rolling, holding the broom handle like a flute and pretending to play it.

I could sometimes picture the priest there, his arms brimming with strange flowers, in a sun hat and a white cassock with a scalloped edge of dried mud, completely absorbed in watching the warm rain fall over the glistening forest. I always saw him smiling. I don't know why.

When I woke in that room in the bishop's palace, I thought of Clémence. I had to get home, at any cost, had to leave straight away, whether the road was passable or not. I would take another route, anything, to get home to her as soon as possible. It wasn't that I had a premonition or was worried. I just wanted her, her skin, her eyes, her kisses, wanted to be near her so that I could forget this feeling of death at work around me.

I put on my clothes which were still damp and splashed my face. Father Lurant was asleep, snoring like a train, his face open and blissful as if he slept in a bed of flowers. I left, on an empty stomach.

Berthe is in the kitchen. I can't see her but I sense her, huffing and blowing, and shaking her head. She always huffs and puffs like that when she sees my notebooks. What difference does it make to her if I spend my days writing in them? She never learned to read. Perhaps it's the marks that frighten her. These sequences of words must seem so mysterious to her, fill her with envy and fear.

I have reached the part that I have been dreading for months. It looms ahead, a hill beyond whose glowering face unknown horrors lurk.

I am getting to the events of that sordid morning. To that moment when the clocks stop and the stars die. The endless fall.

When all is said and done, Berthe is right, words are frightening, even if you can decipher them. Here I am. But I cannot do it. I don't know how to say it. My fingers shake around my pen. My stomach is in knots. My eyes hurt. I am more than fifty years old but I feel as frightened as a child. I drink a glass of wine. Then another, down in one. Then another. I knock it back straight from the bottle, thinking that the words might come out at the same time. Come to me, Clémence. She leans over my shoulder. I feel her young breath on the back of my old grey neck.

'Drinking in the morning, you should be ashamed of yourself. You'll be drunk by noon!'

It's Berthe. I shout at her, tell her to leave me alone, mind her own business. She shrugs her shoulders and goes. I take a deep breath, pick up my pen.

My heart was beating hard when I saw the house, completely covered in snow and dazzling in the dancing sunlight. Icicles stretched from the roof to the white ground. I wasn't cold or hungry any more, forgot the four hours of forced marching along a road crowded with carts, cars and lorries. I had overtaken soldiers in their hundreds, trudging solemnly on, resenting me as I hurried past in my civilian clothes towards the place they themselves didn't want to reach.

Then, at last, I got to the house. Our house. I smacked my stout shoes against the wall, not so much to get rid of the snow as to make a noise, a familiar noise which would let her know I was there, just on the other side of the wall, a few footsteps, a few seconds away. I smiled as I pictured her picturing me. I grasped the handle of the door and pushed, beaming happily. There was no more war, no ghosts, no murdered child. There was just my love, and I was going to be with her, to take her in my arms and run my hands over her tummy and feel the child to be.

I went inside.

An odd thing, you know, this life. Gives you no warning. Everything gets muddled up and you can't sort through it, and moments of blood and pain follow straight on from moments of grace, just like that. It's as if you are one of those tiny pebbles on a road, staying in the same place for days on end, but then kicked into the air by a passing tramp for no reason. Can a pebble alter what happens?

In the house there was a strange silence and my smile vanished. There was also an odd feeling, as if the house had been empty for weeks. Everything was in its place, as usual, but it all felt heavier, colder. And weighing on everything was that silence, pushing the walls apart, drowning my voice when I called. All of a sudden, my heart was racing. I got to the top of the stairs. The bedroom door stood half open. I took two steps forwards. For a moment I could not go in.

I no longer really remember the sequence of things, or what I did. Clémence was on the bed, her forehead pale and her lips paler still. She had lost a lot of blood and her hands gripped her tummy as if she had tried all by herself to deliver into the daylight this creature she had carried for months. The terrible mess around her showed what she had tried to do, how she had struggled, fallen. She had not been able to open the window to call for help, had not dared go down the stairs for fear of falling and losing the child. In the end she had lain on the bed, that battleground of pain. Her breathing was slow, terrifyingly slow, and her cheeks were barely warm. She looked as if life was abandoning her. I put my lips on hers, said her name, screamed her name. I took her face in my hands, slapped her cheeks, blew air into her mouth. Not once did I think of the child. I thought only of her. I too tried to open the window, but the handle came away in my hand, so I punched out one of the panes and cut myself so that my blood mingled with hers. I roared into the street like a mad dog. Doors opened, windows opened. I fell to the ground. I fell and I am falling still. I live only in that fall. Even now.

xvii

Hippolyte Lucy is with Clémence. He's leaning over her with his tense face and all his instruments. They've made me sit down. I watch but I do not understand. There are lots of people in the room. Neighbours, old women, young women, all talking in hushed voices as if this were already a wake. Bitches. Where were they when Clémence was sobbing, when she tried to call for help? Where were they, those females who are feasting now on this pain, under my nose, at my expense! I get up, fists clenched hard, I must look like a madman, a killer, a lunatic. They shrink from me and I throw them out and shut the door on them. There are just the three of us now, Clémence, the doctor and myself.

I have already said that Hippolyte Lucy was a good doctor. A good doctor and a good man. I could not see what he was doing but I knew that he was doing it well. He said some words to me, *haemorrhage, coma*. He asked me to be quick. I lifted Clémence up. She was light as a feather. You would have thought that only her tummy was alive, that life had taken refuge there in that huge, all-consuming famished belly.

I held her close to me in the carriage as the doctor cracked his whip over the haunches of his two old nags. When we got to the hospital, she was taken away from me by two nurses with a trolley. Clémence left in a whiff of ether and a rustling of white sheets. I was told to wait.

I waited for hours, sitting next to a soldier who had lost his left arm. I remember him telling me he was glad to have lost an arm, particularly his left arm, a stroke of luck with him being right-handed. Within a week he would be home for good. Far away from this cuckolds' war, as he called it. An arm for a life. Years of life. He kept on saying it, pointing to where the arm had been. He had even given it a name, his lost arm: Gugusse. And he talked to Gugusse non-stop, asking it to back him up, scolding it, teasing it. Happiness hangs by a thread, no more, or sometimes by an arm. War turns the world upside down. It turns an amputee into the happiest man alive. He was called Léon Castrie, that soldier, and he was from the Morvan. He made me smoke endless cigarettes and had me reeling with all his talk, and I certainly needed it. He did not ask me one single question, did not even ask me to make conversation. He had his lost arm for that. When he finally got up to go he stood and said: 'Well, Gugusse and I had better be getting on!' It was time for a bowl of soup. Léon Castrie, thirty-one years old, a Corporal in the 127th, from the Morvan region, single, a farm labourer. Loved life and cabbage soup. That's all I remember.

I didn't want to go home. I wanted to be there even if I was not doing any good. A nurse came. It was already evening. She told me that the child had been saved, to follow her if I wanted to see him. I shook my head. It was Clémence I wanted to see, I said. Was there news? The nurse told me to wait a bit longer, she would ask the doctor. Then she left.

Later, a doctor came, a military doctor, exhausted, spent, on his last legs. He was dressed like a butcher, a slaughterman, his overall and cap daubed with blood. He had been operating non-stop for days, churning out a constant stream of Gugusses, making some men happy, killing some, mutilating them all. A young woman in this place, among all this male meat seemed wrong to him. He talked to me about the baby

[113]

too, this baby who was too big to come out all on his own. The child was saved. Then he gave me a cigarette. A bad sign. I know those cigarettes only too well. I've offered them to fellows myself when I've known that life, or at the very least freedom, would soon be lost to them. So we smoked for a while without speaking. Then as he exhaled, avoiding my eyes, he murmured: 'She lost too much blood . . .' The words hung in the air between us like the smoke that continued to swirl around us. And that blood he wore, as if buckets of it had been sprayed all over him, was hers, that was Clémence's blood. I looked at the poor chap, saw the bags under his eyes, the three days' worth of stubble on his chin, heard him getting bogged down in his words, and knew that this exhausted man had done everything he could to bring her back to life. And I wanted to kill him. I had never wanted to kill anyone so much. I could have done it with my bare hands. Killed him – savagely, furiously.

'I must get back,' he said, throwing his stub on the ground. Then he touched my murderous arm. 'You can see her,' he said and walked away wearily.

The world does not stop turning because you are suffering. Bastards don't stop being bastards. I have told myself so many times that nothing happens by chance. We are selfish, wrapped up in our own stories. Belle de jour was forgotten, Destinat, Joséphine in her cell, Mierck and Matziev: all forgotten. I should have been there and I was not, and they made the most of it. Those two shits used my absence to cook up their own story to their own liking, in their own good time. You'd almost think they had arranged Clémence's death so as to get rid of me and give themselves some room to manoeuvre. They certainly took advantage of my absence.

You can imagine how news of a crime like the Affaire travels the world. It's like a wave, a stampede, shaking the ground as it passes. People are horrified, but at the same time they like to talk about it. It keeps heads and tongues busy, you could say. For all that, it does no one any good knowing there is a murderer roaming about the countryside, living amongst you, that you might have met him, might come across him, that he might be your neighbour. And when there is a war on, people need to feel that the peacefulness of civilian life is sacrosanct, otherwise everything comes crashing down.

There are only so many ways to end a murder investigation. I know of two: either the guilty man is arrested, or someone who is said to be the guilty man is arrested. It's one or the other. And that's it, in the bag. The public are happy with either ending. The only person who loses out is the one who has been arrested. And who cares what he thinks? If there are more murders, it's different, of course. But, in this case, there was not. Little Belle de jour was the only girl to be strangled. There were no more victims. Proof, for anyone who wanted it, that the accused was indeed the guilty man. Case closed. Hey presto and on we go.

I did not see with my own eyes what I am going to tell you now, but that changes nothing. I spent years gathering these threads together. I've gone over the questions and answers, dug around, retraced steps. This is as close to the truth as you can get. I have invented nothing. Why would I?

On the morning of the third, as I was squelching home, the police arrested two young lads, one of them half dead with cold and hunger. Deserters from the 59th infantry, they were not the first to be scooped up by the boys in blue. For months now we had been watching the exodus begin. They were slipping away from the front like that every day, vanishing into the country-side, preferring sometimes to die alone in the woods and ditches than be blown apart. These two boys were a lucky find, you might say. For everyone. The army wanted to make an example of somebody, and the judge was looking for someone to convict.

The two youngsters were paraded through the streets and people came out to gawp. Two lads, two policemen. Two dirty hairy striplings, uniforms in tatters, faces unshaven, eyes darting in every direction, bellies hollow, footsteps feeble, pinned between two policemen, big strong pink ones, boots waxed, trousers pressed, faces triumphant.

The crowd swelled. No one knew why, a crowd is always a stupid thing, but this one became ugly, closing in around the prisoners. Fists and insults flew, and stones too. These were just harmless country bumpkins if you looked them in the eye. But all together like this, stuck together, sweat and breath smelling, searching faces, on the lookout for the slightest sign or word, they became explosive, like a hellish pressure cooker ready to blow if you so much as touched it.

The policemen could see how the wind was blowing. They walked faster and the deserters started to run. All four took refuge in the *mairie*, where the mayor soon joined them. A period of calm followed. A *mairie* is like a house, a house with a red, white and blue flag outside it. And that fine naïve motto '*Liberté, egalité, fraternité*', beautifully engraved, has a way of cooling things down. The crowd halted and fell silent. And waited. Nothing. After a while the mayor came out and cleared his throat. You could see that his innards were churning with fear. He dabbed his forehead, although it was very cold, and started talking.

'Go home!' he says.

'We want them,' a voice retorts.

'Who do you want?' asks the mayor.

'The killers!' another voice comes in, and the words are immediately picked up by dozens of others, rumbling with menace now.

'What killers?' asks the mayor.

'The girl's killers!' they shout back.

The mayor's mouth falls open in astonishment, then he pulls himself together. He bellows at them that they have gone mad, that they are talking nonsense, raving, that these two men are deserters and will be handed over to the army, because the army knows what to do with them!

'We want them! They did it!' the idiot in the crowd shouts.

'Well, you aren't getting them,' the mayor replies, furious and now mulishly determined. 'And do you know why you aren't getting them? Because the judge has been informed, and he's on his way, and he'll be here soon!'

'Judge' is a magic word. Like 'God' or 'dead' or 'child', words which command respect regardless of your view of them. In addition 'judge' makes you shudder a little, even if you have nothing to feel guilty about, even if you are purer than a white dove. They knew he was talking about Mierck. The business with the eggs had done the rounds and everyone knew how he had spoken of the child, without respect or compassion. Mind you, having said that, even if they did loathe him they feared him; he was still the man whose signature could put you away. The one who rubbed shoulders with the executioner. A bogey man for grown-ups.

The crowd started to fall apart, slowly, then quickly, as if they were all suddenly gripped by an urgent need to piss. Only a dozen or so stayed, stubborn as posts. The mayor turned his back on them and went indoors.

It had been a good idea, waving that word about to scare the crows. A stroke of genius. Otherwise there might well have been a lynching. All the mayor had to do now was call for the judge, something he had of course not yet done.

By the time Mierck arrived, accompanied by Matziev, it was early afternoon. The two men were talking as if they had known each other for years, which does not surprise me because I had already seen them together, and I saw them again later. They were carved from the same rotten branch, as I said. They made their way to the *mairie*, which had been transformed into a fortress by the addition of a dozen specially drafted policemen. First off, the judge ordered two good armchairs to be put in front of the fire in the mayor's office, wine and something to go with it, meaning cheese and white bread. Louisette was sent off to do what she could.

Matziev took out one of his cigars. Mierck looked at his watch, whistling to himself. The mayor just stood there, not really knowing what to do. Then Mierck nodded, which the mayor understood to mean he should fetch the two soldiers and their guards.

The poor lads came into the room, and the blazing fire put

some colour back in their cheeks. Matziev told the policemen to go and mind their own business outside, which made Mierck laugh. They examined the poor boys for a long time. I say boys, because that is almost what they were. The elder, Maurice Rifolon was twenty-two, born in Melun, lived in Paris, 15 rue des Amandiers, in the 20th Arrondissement, a typesetter by trade. The younger, Yann Le Floc, was twenty, born in Plouzagen, a Breton village which he had never left until the war, a farm boy.

'What struck me,' the mayor said to me later, much later, 'was how different they were. The little Breton boy kept his head down. You could see he was terrified. The other one, the typesetter, looked us right in the eye, and almost smiled but not quite. As if he didn't give a damn.'

The officer launched the first attack. 'Do you know why you're here?' he asked.

Rifolon looked him up and down, and gave no reply. The little Breton raised his head slightly. 'Because we left, sir, because we ran away . . .' he mumbled.

Which is when Mierck dived in. 'Because you have killed.'

The little Breton opened his eyes wide. The other one, Rifolon, said quite casually: 'Of course we've killed. That's what we were meant to do. Kill the other boys, the ones who look like our brothers. We kill them and they kill us. It was your lot that told us to do it.'

The little Breton panicked. 'I'm not sure I killed anyone, maybe I didn't, maybe I missed, you can't see very well, and I'm not a good shot. Corporal makes fun of me. "Le Floc," he says, "you'd miss a cow in a corridor!" So, I'm not sure, I might not have killed anyone!'

The officer went over to them. He took a long drag on his cigar, blew the smoke in their faces. The little one coughed. The other did not flinch.

'It was a child that you killed. A girl of ten . . .'

The little one was startled. 'What? what? what?' he said it at least twenty times, hopping on the spot, squirming as if he were on fire. As for the typesetter, he still smiled his calm smile. The judge turned to him.

'You don't seem surprised?'

He took his time to reply, looking the two of them over from head to foot. 'You'd have thought he was weighing them up and finding something funny about it!' the mayor told me. Eventually he said: 'Nothing surprises me any more. If you'd seen what I've been seeing all these months, you'd know that anything can happen.' A well-turned sentence, I would say, and a slap in the judge's face. He went crimson.

'Are you denying it?' he shouted.

'I admit it,' the other man replied calmly.

'What?' the little one shrieked, clutching his friend's collar. 'Have you gone mad, what are you saying? Don't listen to him. I don't know him. We've only been together since last night! I don't know what he's done! The bastard. Why're you doing this? Tell them, tell them!'

Mierck pushed him into a corner of the office as if to say 'we'll see about you in a minute,' and went back to the other man.

'Do you admit it?'

'Whatever you want,' the other man said, quite serenely.

'And the girl?'

'I killed her. It was me. I saw her. I followed her. I stabbed her three times in the back.'

'No, you strangled her.'

'Yes, of course, I strangled her. With these hands right here, you're right, I didn't have a knife.'

'On the banks of the canal.'

'That's right.'

'And you put her in the water.'

'Yes.'

'Why did you do that?'

'Because I felt like . . .'

'Raping her?'

'Yes.'

'But she wasn't raped.'

'Didn't have time. There was a noise. I ran off.'

It was as if he was speaking a part, the mayor said. The typesetter stood very straight, to attention, spoke distinctly. The judge lapped it up. You would have thought they had rehearsed it. The little Breton was crying and shaking his head, his face streaming with snot, his shoulders heaving. Matziev shrouded him in cigar smoke.

'Will you bear witness to this confession?' the judge asked the mayor. The mayor was slumped in a chair. He knew that the typesetter was playing with the judge. And he knew that Mierck knew it. And to cap it all he knew that the judge was also playing. He had what he wanted. A confession.

'Can we really call it a confession . . .' the mayor began, but Matziev stepped into the dance.

'You have ears, sir, and a brain. You must have heard and understood.'

'Perhaps you would like to lead the enquiry?' the judge joined in a sarcastic tone. The mayor said nothing.

The little Breton was still crying. The other still stood to attention, smiling. He was gone already, he was far away. He had done his sums: deserter equals firing squad; murderer equals guillotine. Either way, he was a goner. Goodbye, world! All he wanted was to go quickly. And if he could bugger it up for everyone else while he was at it . . . job well done.

Mierck had the typesetter taken off to a little cell, a broom cupboard of a room on the first floor. A policeman stood guard outside the door.

The judge and the colonel allowed themselves a little break here, and made it clear to the mayor that he would be called if they needed him. The snivelling little Breton was taken away to the cellar, and put in chains because the cellar could not be locked. The rest of the squad was sent back to go over the crime scene with a fine-tooth comb.

It was already well on in the afternoon. Louisette came back with quantities of food she had managed to requisition. The mayor told her to prepare the meal and to serve the gentlemen, and to take a little something to the prisoners. He was not unkind.

'My brother was at the front at the time,' Louisette told me, 'I knew it was hard. He'd thought about giving it all up, too, of coming home. "You could hide me!" he said once when he was on leave, and I told him I wouldn't, that if he did that I'd tell the mayor and the police. I wouldn't have done it though, but I was frightened that he really would desert, that he'd be caught and shot. In the end, he died anyway, a week before the armistice . . . So you see, those poor boys, I felt sorry for them, so before I fed the two who didn't need feeding, I went down to the prisoners. I gave bread and bacon to the one in the cellar, but he didn't want it. He was all huddled up, crying like a baby. I left it for him. Then I went to the other one. I knocked on the door, there was no reply, I knocked again. No reply. My hands were full with the bread and bacon so the policeman opened the door for me, and then we saw him. He was smiling, poor boy, I swear he was smiling, looking us right in the face, eyes wide open. I screamed, and everything fell on the floor, the policeman said "Shit!" and jumped for him but it was too late, he was good and dead. He did it with his trousers, ripped them into strips and tied them to the window latch. I wouldn't have thought a window latch would hold . . .'

When they heard the news, Mierck and Matziev were

unperturbed. 'More proof!' they told the mayor. And they looked at each other knowingly.

Night was falling. Matziev put some logs on the fire, and the judge called for Louisette. She arrived, very shaken, thinking they were going to question her about the hanged man. Instead Mierck asked her what she had found by way of food. She said: 'Three sausages, some *rillettes*, ham, pig's trotters, a chicken, some calves' liver, and a goat's cheese.' The judge's face lit up. 'Good, very good,' he said to her, his mouth watering. He placed his order: charcuterie to start, then braised liver, hotpot of chicken with cabbage, carrots, onions and sausage, followed by stewed pig's trotters, then cheese and then pancakes with apples. And wine of course, the best: white to start, then red. He waved her off to the kitchen.

Louisette spent the whole evening between the *mairie* and the mayor's house, wine and dishes coming one way, empty bottles and plates the other. The mayor was at home in bed, struck down by a sudden fever. The typesetter had been taken to the morgue at the hospital. Only one policeman was left to stand guard over the little Breton. His name was Louis Despiaux. He was a good sort. I will come back to him later.

The judge and the colonel had installed themselves in the mayor's office overlooking a little courtyard where a scrawny chestnut tree which had not quite decided whether or not it would become a proper tree reached pathetically for the sky. It went a long time ago, chopped down on the mayor's orders. He could not bear to look at it after the *Affaire*, it always reminded him of something else. You could get from the office into the little courtyard through a door in a corner of the room. The door was painted with the spines of books, a kind of trompe-l'oeil, and very effective. It made the real book-shelves, where the unopened and the unread shared space with great legal tomes, look less sparsely populated. At the far end of the courtyard there were some privies and a narrow awning under which firewood was stacked.

There was a shout when Louisette brought in the ham and *rillettes*, not an angry one but an expression of contentment. Matziev made some joke, she doesn't remember exactly what, but it was at her expense, and it made the judge laugh. She laid the round table with plates, cutlery, glasses, all the trimmings, and then she served up the first course. The officer threw his cigar into the fire and was the first to take his place. He asked her what her name was. 'Louisette,' she replied. He said, 'A very pretty name for a very pretty girl.' And Louisette smiled, and popped the compliment in her pocket, not realising that he was making fun of her with her missing front teeth and her squint. Then the judge asked her to go down to the cellar and tell the policeman that they wanted to speak to the prisoner. Louisette was shaking as she went down, as if she were going into Hell itself. The little Breton had stopped crying but he had not touched the bread and bacon she had left for him. The policeman told the prisoner that he had to go, and when there was no reaction he grabbed him by his chains and led him off.

'It was very damp in the cellar.' We were sitting on the terrace of the Café de la Croix in V on a mild June evening, and Despiaux was recalling that wretched evening for me. I tracked Despiaux down quite recently. He left the police force after it all happened, and headed south, to a brother-in-law who tended a vineyard. From there he went to Algeria to work for a maritime trading company. He came back to V at the beginning of '21 and at this point was working in the accounts department of Carbonnieux, the big shop. A good position, he said. He was a tall man, finely built but not thin, and his face was still very young but his hair was as white as flour. It went white all at once, after that night. The emptiness in his eyes is so deep you are tempted to explore, but you hesitate for fear of losing yourself.

'The boy hadn't spoken a word to me the whole time. He'd cried his heart out, then nothing. I told him we had to go up. When we got to the mayor's office it was like the Sahara, so hot, like an oven. The grate was banked up with enough logs for three fires, all blazing red like a cock's comb. The colonel and the judge were sitting down, their mouths full of food and their glasses in their hands. I saluted them and they tilted their glasses slightly in return. I didn't know what I was getting into.'

When the little Breton saw those two enjoying themselves he woke up a bit, started to sob, then he started again with his 'What? What?' This deflated Mierck a bit, ruined his mood. Between mouthfuls of rillettes, he flung the news of the typesetter's death at the little Breton, quite casually, and the lad, who knew nothing till then – and nor in fact did Despiaux – looked as if someone had thrown a stone in his face. He staggered and almost fell back, but Despiaux caught him.

'You see,' the officer said, 'your accomplice couldn't cope with what you've done. So he took his life.'

'He had some honour, at least,' added the judge. 'What are you waiting for? Tell us everything!'

There was a short silence. According to Despiaux, the boy looked at him, then at Mierck, then at Maztiev, and then he began to wail, a sound the like of which no one had ever heard. Despiaux didn't know that a man could make a noise like that, and the worst of it was it went on and on. He would not stop. Where did this terrible noise come from? What stopped it, though, was when Colonel Matziev whipped him right across the face. He actually stood up specially to do it. The little Breton stopped all at once. A long purple weal ran right down his face, little beads of blood standing out in places. With a tilt of his head, Mierck ordered the boy to be taken back down to the cellar. Despiaux was about to do so when Matziev's voice stopped him.

'I've got a better idea,' he said. 'Take him out into the courtyard to cool off a bit – it might help him remember.'

'The courtyard?' Despiaux asked.

'Yes, the courtyard,' Matziev relied, waving to the window. 'There's even something to tie him up to. Get on with it!'

'Sir, it's just that . . . it's very cold, it must be freezing,' Despiaux ventured.

'Do as you're told!' barked the judge, ripping a mouthful of ham from the bone.

'I was twenty-two,' Despiaux told me, as we ordered another round of Pernods. 'What can you say at twenty-two, what can you do? I took the boy into the courtyard and tied him to the chestnut tree. It must have been about nine o'clock. We went from the office where the heat could have killed you out into the dark and the frost. It was minus ten, minus twelve maybe. I didn't feel proud of myself. The boy was crying. "If you did it you'd be better off telling them everything, then it'll all be over and you'll be back in the warm", I said in his ear. "But it wasn't me, it wasn't me," he chanted under his breath. The courtyard was in total darkness. There were dozens of stars up in the sky and in front of us was the window to the mayor's office, silhouetted like the stage of a toy theatre, and we watched the scene, two men, not a care in the world, with bright red faces, eating and drinking round a table laden with food.

'I went back into the office but Matziev told me to wait in the next room. He said they'd call me. I sat down on a sort of bench and waited, fiddling with my hands and wondering what I should do. I could see the courtyard from the window of that room too, could see the prisoner tied to the tree. I stayed there in the dark, didn't feel like putting the light on, didn't want him to see me. I was ashamed. I wanted to run away, to get out of there, but with my uniform I couldn't. You have to respect the uniform. If it was now, it would be different, that's for sure! Every now and then I heard their voices, laughter, heard the footsteps of the mayor's servant as she brought them in more steaming, wonderful-smelling dishes – except that that night the smell was like a terrible stench you couldn't get out of your nose. I had a lead weight in my stomach. I was ashamed to call myself a man.'

Louisette made many trips back and forth. 'And it was so cold you wouldn't have put a dog out!' she told me. The supper went on for two hours. Mierck and Matziev were in no hurry. They savoured every minute of it, the meal and everything. Louisette has a habit of keeping her eyes on her feet and that night she was more than usually bashful, barely looking up. 'They frightened me, the two of them, and they were beginning to get drunk!' She didn't look at the little Breton down in the courtyard. Sometimes it is more convenient not to see.

From time to time, Matziev would go out to speak to the prisoner, just a few words, leaning close to him and speaking into his ear. The boy shivered and moaned, protesting that it was not him, that he had done nothing. The officer would shrug his shoulders, rub his hands and blow on them. He would shiver with the cold, and hurry back into the warmth. Despiaux saw it all from his place by the window, transfixed in the dark as if he too were tied up.

Towards midnight, Mierck's and Matziev's lips were glistening with pork jelly as they finished the cheese. Their talk got louder and louder, they were singing and banging the table. Six bottles of wine had been drunk. Just the six.

They went out into the courtyard, 'to get some fresh air'. It was Mierck's first visit to the prisoner, Matziev's fifth. They walked round him as if he did not exist, Mierck looking up at the sky and talking about the stars in a conversational way, naming them and pointing them out for Matziev. Astronomy was one of his passions, 'In our weakness they console us, so pure . . .' Despiaux heard it all, their talk and the chattering of the prisoner's teeth, like pebbles thrown against a wall. Matziev took out a cigar and offered it to the judge, who declined. For a while they carried on talking about the stars and the movement of the planets, looking up into the distant vault of the sky. Then, as if someone had pricked them, they suddenly turned to the prisoner.

He had been out in the cold for three hours by then. He, poor boy, had had plenty of time to look at the stars, before his tears froze his eyelids together.

The officer trailed the glowing tip of his cigar under the boy's nose and asked him the question again. The boy replied only with a moan. After a while Matziev became annoyed.

'Are you a man or a beast?' he bellowed in his ear. Still no reply. Matziev threw his cigar in the snow, grabbed the prisoner and shook him while Mierck stood watching and blowing on his fingers. Matziev let the Breton's shivering body drop, then started looking around. He found nothing, but an idea, a true bastard's idea, began brewing in his corrupt head.

'Are you still a bit warm, is that it?' he said in the boy's ear. 'I'll cool you down a bit, my lad!' And he took a hunting knife from his pocket and opened the blade. He sliced the buttons from the boy's tunic, one by one, quite methodically, then he started on his shirt, then his vest. He took the boy's clothes off carefully. His bare chest glowed pale in the shadowy courtyard.

When he had finished with the top half, he set about the bottom half, trousers, long johns, underpants. He sliced through the boy's laces, took off his shoes slowly, whistling 'Caroline and her little patent shoes'. The boy was shaking his head like a madman and yelling. When Matziev stood back, the prisoner was completely naked.

'Better now? D'you feel more comfortable? It'll all come back to you now, I'm sure.'

He turned to the judge, who said: 'Let's go in. I'm freezing.'

They laughed at the joke and went in to Louisette's steaming apple pancakes, coffee, and the bottle of plum brandy.

Despiaux looked up at the June sky, breathed in its warmth. Night was sneaking up on us. I was listening to him, and keeping our glasses topped up. There were lots of people around us on the terrace, having fun and laughing, but we were alone there, and we were cold.

'I was by the window, a little back from it,' Despiaux went on. 'I couldn't take my eyes off him. He had rolled into a ball like a dog at the foot of the tree, and I could see him shaking, shivering convulsively. I wept. I swear it, I cried and couldn't stop myself. Then the boy started making noises like an animal, like they say the wolves used to when there were still wolves in the forests, on and on, and the judge and Matziev laughed all the louder. I could hear them in the next room. That boy's cries bit into my heart.'

I can just see them, Mierck and Matziev, standing with their noses up against the window, their backsides towards the fire, brandy glasses in their hands, bellies about to burst, and their eyes on the naked boy squirming in the frost, and going on talking about hare coursing and astronomy or book-binding. That's only how I imagine the scene, but I don't think I am wrong.

What I do know is that a little later Despiaux saw the officer go outside again. He nudged the prisoner with the tip of his boot, three times, three little kicks in the back and the stomach, as you would do to check if a dog was dead or not. The boy reached for the boot, perhaps to beg, but Matziev pushed him away, and ground his heel down on the boy's face. He moaned, then he howled all the louder as the officer poured a jug of water over him.

'His voice, his voice, if you could have heard his voice. It wasn't really a voice any more. And what he was saying, the words, they came out all jumbled up and didn't seem to mean anything. And then at the end of it he started shouting, shouting that it was him, it was *him*, he admitted everything, the crime, every crime, he had killed, he had *really* killed . . . There was no holding him back then.'

Despiaux put his glass down on the table. He looked into the bottom of it as if it might give him the strength to continue.

Matziev had called him down. The boy was writhing about, still saying the same thing over and over again: 'I did it, I did it, I did it!' His skin was blue, patched with red in places, the tips of his fingers and toes already going black, but his face was as white as a dying man's. Despiaux wrapped him in a blanket and helped him inside. Matziev went back up to Mierck and they toasted their success: the cold had done its job. Despiaux could not stop the boy talking now. He gave him something to drink, something warm, but he could not swallow. Despiaux watched over him all night; there was nothing left to guard. There was nothing left any more.

A June evening almost makes you think there is hope for us all; for this world and for all humanity. The air is full of such perfume, of girls and trees and things, and so lovely that you feel you could start again, rub your eyes and rub out the evil; pain is only a trick played by the soul. Perhaps that's why I suggested a bite to eat somewhere. Despiaux looked at me as if I had sworn at him, and shook his head. Perhaps raking over the ashes had made him lose his appetite. I wasn't really hungry either, but didn't want us to go our separate ways too soon. Before I had time to order another round, Despiaux stood up, unfurling his long body, smoothing his jacket with both hands. He straightened his hat and looked me right in the eye. It was the first time he had looked at me like that, with a touch of bitterness.

'And you,' he said, his voice sharp with reproach. 'Where were you that night?'

I sat there, in stupid silence. Clémence came to my side. I looked at her, just as lovely, transparent but lovely. What could I tell him? He was waiting for a reply. I sat there with my mouth open, looking at him, looking at the space beside me where I alone could see Clémence. Despiaux shrugged his shoulders, tugged his hat and turned his back on me without a goodbye. He walked away. He left to go back to his own regrets, leaving me to mine.

I knew Madame de Flers by sight. She came from a very old V family, and was well born, like Destinat. Her husband, Major de Flers, had fallen straight away in September 1914. I can remember being unkind, thinking that widowhood would suit her like a couture gown, and that she would use it to raise her position at table. I can be as foolish and bitter as the next man. In fact, she left V and her palatial home, and presented herself at the hospital in our town. She wanted to be useful. People said: 'She won't last three days, she'll faint at the sight of blood and shit!'

She lasted. Despite the blood and the shit. She made people forget her fortune and her noble name with her boundless goodness and her simplicity. She slept in a maid's room and spent her days and nights by the bedsides of the dying and those brought back from the dead. War kills: it massacres, mutilates, sullies, dirties, disembowels, separates, crushes, hacks and kills. But sometimes it sets the pendulum right.

Madame de Flers took me by the hand and I let myself be led to Clémence. She kept saying she was sorry. 'We have no private rooms, nowhere . . .'

We went into a huge ward where the air was filled with groans and the acrid smell of dirty bandages. This was how the wounded smelled. Death is different, more horrible, more strident. There were perhaps thirty beds in the ward, forty even, all full, and on some of them I could make out the movement of bandaged shapes. In the middle of the room there was a kind of cubicle made of four white sheets which swayed gently. That was where Clémence was, in the middle of this room full of soldiers who were not aware of her, no more than she was of them.

Madame de Flers held aside one of the sheets, and I saw. She was lying with her eyes closed, her hands laid across her chest, as if resting. Her breathing was majestically slow, her chest rising, swelling but leaving her features impassive. I fell on to a chair by the bed. Madame de Flers laid her hand on Clémence's forehead and stroked it, then she said: 'The child is doing well.' I looked at her and couldn't understand her. Then she said: 'I'll leave you, stay as long as you like.' She drew the curtain aside like an actor and stepped behind it.

I stayed beside Clémence all night. I watched her, could not stop watching her. I did not dare speak to her for fear that one of the injured men around us might hear. I laid my hand on her, to draw warmth from her and to give her mine. I was sure that she could feel my presence, and would draw strength from it, and give some back to me. She was beautiful, a little paler than when I had left her the day before, but softer too, as if the deep sleep in which she was drifting had driven away all concern, all worries. Yes, she was beautiful.

I would never see her ugly, old, lined and worn. I have lived all these years with a woman who has never grown old: while I crumble, she remains unchanged, irreproachable. Nothing can take that from me, even if time has robbed me of her face. I struggle to remember it, though sometimes I catch a glimpse of her in a glass of wine. Some recompense.

All through the night the soldier in the bed nearest Clémence rambled and stammered. Sometimes he sang, or got angry, but his voice stayed the same. I couldn't tell who he thought he was talking to – a friend, a relation, a sweetheart, himself – but he covered all topics: the war of course, but other more mundane things, meadows to mow, roofs to mend, wedding breakfasts, drowned cats, trees covered in caterpillars, embroidered linen, ploughs, altar boys, floods, mattresses borrowed and never returned, wood to chop. A kaleidoscope, constantly shuffling and serving up the episodes of his life in any old older, making one absurd story out of it – just as life does, in fact. One name came up over and over again, Albert Jivonal. I think it was his own name, that he needed to say it aloud, perhaps to prove to himself that he was still alive.

He was like the first violin in the symphony of the dying. Death rattled all around us: the laboured breathing of those who had been gassed, the plaintive moans and crazed laughter, the whispered names of women and mothers, and, rising above it all, this litany of Jivonal's. It was as if we were adrift, Clémence and I, with me keeping watch as we sailed an invisible ship on the river of the dead, like in the stories we used to get at school when we would listen wide-eyed, fear in our veins, while outside darkness was already falling like a cloak of black wool on the shoulders of a giant.

Towards morning, Clémence stirred, unless exhaustion made me see things. I believe that her face turned towards me slightly. What I know is that she breathed harder and longer than she had before. A great breath, like the beautiful sigh when something long awaited has finally arrived and you want to show your pleasure. I put my hand on her throat. I knew. Sometimes we surprise ourselves with things we know but have never learned. I knew that this sigh was her last. There would be no more. I laid my head alongside hers and stayed there for a long time, felt the warmth gradually leaving her. I prayed to God and the angels for the dream to end.

Albert Jivonal died shortly after Clémence. He fell silent

and I knew he was dead. I hated him. When he stepped into death he would find himself near her in that infinite queue. Where he was now, he could probably see her, just a few metres ahead of him. Even though I did not know him, and never saw his face, I hated him. I was jealous of a dead man. I should have had his place.

The day nurse came in at seven o'clock and closed Clémence's eyes, because, strangely, she had opened them at the moment of death. I stayed there for a long time and no one dared tell me to leave. I did leave, though, all on my own. And there you have it.

Belle de jour was buried in V a week after the murder. I did not attend, I had pain of my own, but I heard that the church was full to bursting and that there were another hundred or so people in the little square outside, despite the lashing rain. The Prosecutor was there. So was the judge. And Matziev. Bourrache of course, and his wife, who had to be held up, and the sisters, Aline and Rose, who seemed not to understand what was happening. Adélaïde Siffert, Belle's godmother, was there too, bleating on and on to everyone at the graveside, 'If only I'd known . . . if only I'd known.' The problem is, you never know.

When it was our turn, there were not many in the church. I say 'our' because it felt to me as if we were still together, even if I was standing and Clémence was lying in the oak coffin surrounded by candles. Even if I could no longer see her or feel her. Father Lurant said the mass, his words simple and fitting. I remembered the man with whom I had shared a meal and a room while Clémence was dying.

I had fallen out with my father long before, and Clémence had no family left. A good thing too. I could not have borne being taken under any wings, or being obliged to talk or listen, being kissed, or held in someone's arms, or pitied. I wanted to be alone. And it might as well begin at once, for I was to be alone now for life.

At the graveside, there were just six of us: the priest, Ostrane the gravedigger, Clémentine Hussard, Léocadie Renaut, Marguerite Bonsergent (three old ladies who went to all the funerals), and myself. Father Lurant said the last prayer and we listened, heads bowed, and Ostrane rested his calloused hands on the handle of his shovel. I looked at the countryside, the meadow that stretched down to the Guerlante, the naked trees and the dirty brown footpaths on the hillside, the heavy sky. The old women threw flowers onto the coffin and the priest made the sign of the cross as Ostrane picked up his shovel. I left. I did not want to see.

That night I dreamed of Clémence under the earth and she was crying. Beasts with hideous faces, fangs and claws were attacking her, and she was shielding her face with her hands but they kept on coming and eventually they reached her, and began to eat, biting off fine strips of her flesh, which they swallowed. Clémence kept saying my name. She had sand and roots in her mouth, and her eyes were empty, white and lifeless.

I woke with a start, soaked, gasping for breath. Then I saw that I was alone in the bed. How big, how naked a bed can be. I thought of her under the earth, on her first night of exile, and I cried like a child.

Days followed, I have no idea how many. And nights. I stopped going out. I wavered. I hesitated. I would take Gachentard's gun, put a bullet in the magazine, drive the barrel into my mouth. I was drunk from dawn till dusk. The house started to smell like a festering ditch. I drew all my strength from the bottle. Sometimes I would punch the walls. Neighbours came but I turned them away. The face of a castaway stared back at me from the mirror. And then one morning, a nun from the hospital came knocking at the door. In her arms was a little bundle of cloth which moved feebly. The child. But I will talk about that when I have finished with the others, not now.

XX

Mierck had had the little Breton locked up in the prison at V, even though the army said it wanted him for the firing squad. It was now a case of who would get to bump him off first. Even so, it took time. Enough for me to get to see him. By then he had been in prison for six weeks.

The prison had been a monastery once, and dated back to the Middle Ages. There were prisoners now instead of monks but otherwise not much had changed. The refectory was still the refectory, the cells, cells. They had added a few iron bars, some locked doors, and they had stuck barbed metal stakes along the walls. Very little light seeped through. Even on bright days it was dark in there. As you stepped inside it, you had only one thought and that was to run back out as quickly as possible.

I told them that the judge had sent me, but no one checked. They knew me.

When the guard opened the door to the Breton's cell, I could not see much at first, but I heard him straight away, singing, in a quiet childlike voice. Rather a lovely voice in fact. The guard closed the door behind us and as my eyes grew accustomed to the gloom I caught sight of him, sitting in a corner, knees drawn up to his chin, head rolling as he sang. It was the first time I had seen him, and he looked even younger than his years, with beautiful blond hair, and blue eyes which stared at the floor. I didn't know if he heard me come in but when I spoke to him he did not seem surprised.

'So, did you really kill her? Did you kill the little girl?'

He stopped, without looking up, and sang to the same tune: 'I did, I really did, I did, I really did . . .'

I said: 'I'm not the judge, or Matziev. Don't be afraid. You can tell me.'

He looked at me then with an absent smile that came from far, far away, moving his head like a cherub in a coin-fed crib at Christmas. And without another word he launched into his song again with its 'ripe corn, skylarks, weddings and posies'.

I stayed there a little longer. Those hands, I wondered, were they the hands of a killer? When I left, he did not turn his head, just carried on singing and rocking. A month and a half later, after appearing before the military tribunal charged with desertion and murder, he was found guilty on both counts and shot almost in the same breath.

The *Affaire* was closed.

In one night, Mierck and Matziev had created a madman, and a perfect and consenting criminal, out of one little peasant. I only found out later, when I had tracked down Despiaux, what had happened that wretched night. What I did already know, though, was that neither the judge nor Matziev had spoken to the Prosecutor. Joséphine's words had been summarily forgotten. I have often wondered why. After all, Mierck definitely loathed Destinat, and this was the perfect opportunity to pester him and to drag his patrician face through the mud.

Some things are stronger than hate. There are rules. Destinat and Mierck belonged to the same world, the world of the well-born, of lace-trimmed upbringings, of hand-kissing and motor cars, of wainscotting and money. Beyond facts and feelings, beyond law, there was complicity: 'You don't bother me, and I don't bother you'. Believing that one of your own kind could be a murderer is like believing that you yourself could be. Men like that who look down on the rest of us as if we were chicken shit, would have to accept that they have rotten corrupted souls, just as we do. That they are like us. And that would be the beginning of the end of their world. Inconceivable.

Why would Destinat have killed Belle de jour? He might have spoken to her, yes. But killed her?

When the Breton was arrested they found a five-franc note in his pocket with a little cross pencilled on the top left-hand corner. Adélaïde Siffert formally identified it as the note she had given to her goddaughter that awful Sunday. Those crosses on banknotes were an obsession of hers, something she always did to prove that the notes were hers.

The deserter swore that he had found it beside the canal. So he *was* there! Yes, and so what? What does it prove? They had slept there, the typesetter and himself, under the *Boudin*, the famous whitewashed bridge, huddled together out of the snow and wind. The police had seen the flattened outlines of two bodies in the grass. He admitted that too without any difficulty.

On the other side of the little canal, more or less opposite the place where the little door opens onto the grounds of the château, stands the factory laboratory, a great framework of glass lit up day and night. The monster never sleeps. There must always be two engineers in the laboratory at any time to check the proportions and the quality of what comes out of its arse.

When I asked to speak to whoever was on duty on the night of the crime, Arsène Meyer, the personnel manager, looked at the pencil he had in his hand and twiddled it round and round.

'Is the answer on your pencil, then?' I asked him. We had known each other a long time, and he owed me a favour. I had turned a blind eye in 1915 when his eldest son, a real jackass, had thought he could help himself to all the army equipment that was stored near the Place de la Liberté – the blankets, mess tins and rations. I gave the fool a dressing-down and he put everything back where it came from. No report was filed and no one ever knew.

'They're not here any more . . .' Meyer said.

'Since when?' I asked him.

He looked at his pencil again and mumbled something I had to strain to hear. 'They went to England, nearly two months ago.'

England was nearly the other side of the world, particularly when the war was on. And two months ago meant shortly after the crime.

'Why did they leave?'

'They were told to.'

'Who told them?'

'The director.'

'And was this departure expected? Was it planned?'

Meyer's pencil broke. He was sweating. 'You'd better leave,' he told me, 'I have my orders, and you may be an investigator, but you're small fry next to them.'

I did not want to needle him further so I left him to his discomfort, thinking that I would go and speak to the director himself the following day.

I did not have time. Next day someone came at dawn with a message for me. The judge wanted to see me, at once. I knew why. How quickly news spreads.

As usual, I was greeted by Crusty, and made to hang around in the anteroom for a good hour. I could hear voices through the padded leather door, cheerful voices. When Crusty came back to tell me that the judge was ready to receive me, I was busy tearing a strip of red silk away from the wall with my finger. I had taken off a good forty centimetres. The clerk looked at me with some surprise and distress, the way you look at someone who is not well, but he said nothing and I followed him.

Mierck was lolling in his armchair. Beside him stood Matziev, like a slimmer, taller version. They never left each other's side now, like twin souls, as if they had fallen in love. Matziev was extending his stay at Bassepin's house and driving us to distraction with his phonograph. We had to wait until the end of January before he pissed off and left us in peace, never to show his face again.

Mierck did not beat about the bush. 'On what authority did you go to the factory?' he barked.

I gave no reply.

'What are you looking for? The *Affaire* has been resolved, and the guilty men have paid!'

'So I have been told,' I replied, making him even tetchier.

'What? What are you insinuating?'

'I'm not insinuating anything. I'm doing my job.'

Matziev was fiddling with an unlit cigar as Mierck set off on his attack again, like a bullock with its balls trapped between two bricks.

'Precisely. Do your job, and leave law-abiding citizens in peace. If I hear that you have been asking any more questions in relation to this case, which has been judged and closed, I will disbar you.' His voice became gentler. 'I understand that in the present circumstances you may not be entirely yourself, with your wife's death, it must be hard . . .'

Hearing him talking about Clémence that way was like trying to pretty up a heap of cow dung with a sprig of jasmine.

'Shut up,' I said.

His eyes popped open and he flushed scarlet and said furiously: 'What? You dare give *me* orders? *You?*'

'Bugger off!' I replied.

Mierck almost fell off his chair. Matziev looked me up and down, and said nothing. He lit his cigar and then shook the match for much longer than necessary.

Out in the street the sun was shining. I felt slightly drunk, and I would have really liked to talk to someone, someone I could trust and who saw things the way I did. I do not mean just about the *Affaire*. I mean life, the weather, everything and nothing.

I thought of Mazerulles, the inspector's secretary at the Education Department. It would do me good to see his grey turnip face again, the look he had in his eye, like a wet dog waiting to be patted. I started to head towards the Place des Carmes where the department's offices were. I was in no hurry. A weight had been lifted from me, and I could still see the expression on Mierck's face when I had told him to bugger off. He was probably already demanding my head. What did I care?

When I asked the *concierge* whether Mazerulles still worked there, he caught his glasses, which had a way of falling off. 'Monsieur Mazerulles left us a year ago,' he told me.

'Is he still in V?' I asked.

The man looked at me as if I had just landed from the moon. 'I don't think he will have moved from the cemetery, but you could always go and check.'

XXI

Weeks slipped by and spring came round again. I went to Clémence's grave twice a day, every day, morning and evening. I told her how my hours were spent, as if she were still beside me, just in an ordinary way, where words of love need no polishing to shine like gold coins.

I thought about dropping everything and leaving. But then I remembered that the world was round, and it would not be long before I came back to where I had started. Stupid really. I half relied on Mierck forcing my hand. I told myself he would want revenge, that he would find a way to have me moved on. The truth is I was a coward. I left decisions to others. Mierck did nothing, or at least nothing that worked.

It was 1918. You could smell the war coming to an end – easy to say now with hindsight, but I am telling the truth. You could smell it, and it made those last convoys all the more unbearable. Our little town was still full of the lame and disfigured, stitched back together as best they could be. The hospital was full, like a prestigious hotel in a spa resort, much sought-after by those in the know. Except that the high season had been going on for four years. Sometimes I would catch sight of Madame de Flers in the distance and it made my heart pound.

Every day, or nearly, I would go to the banks of the canal, like a stubborn dog (or a mad one), not to find a clue but to keep the whole thing alive. Often I could sense Destinat on the other side of the garden wall, and I knew that he saw me there. Since his retirement he rarely left his house, and received even fewer visitors. In other words, he received no one. He spent his days in silence, not even reading, sitting at his desk with his hands clasped together or looking out of the window. He'd wander his grounds, Barbe told me, like a lone animal. We were not unalike, he and I, when you came down to it.

One day, 13 June 1918, when I was walking along the banks and had just passed the *Boudin*, I heard a rustling of grass behind me. I turned round. It was him. Taller even than I remembered him, hair so grey it was almost white, smoothed back from his forehead. He wore a black suit and his shoes were polished, and in his right hand he held an ivory-topped cane. I think he had come out of the door at the end of the garden and was waiting for me to come past.

We looked at each other for a long time, without a word, the way big cats gauge each other before the attack, or like old friends who have been long apart. I must have looked pitiful. Those few months had hollowed out my frame and my features more than ten years could have done.

Destinat spoke first. 'I often see you here, you know . . .'

He let the sentence dangle; perhaps he couldn't or wouldn't finish it. It was such a long time since I had spoken to him that I was no longer quite sure how you went about it.

He delved through the moss on the edge of the canal with the tip of his cane, came a little closer to me and scrutinised me, very closely. It's strange, but having his eyes on me like that felt almost like a blessing, soothing and calm, like when an old doctor who has known you since childhood examines you. It was the oddest thing.

'You have never asked me . . .'

Again he did not finish the sentence. I saw his lips quiver and his eyelids flutter briefly in the light. I knew what he meant to say. We understood each other.

'Would you have answered?' I said, dragging my words out the way he did.

He took a deep breath and jangled his watch which hung on the end of a little chain to which a strange black key was also attached. Then he looked into the distance, to the sky which was a very light blue, but his eyes quickly came back to me and bored into mine, so that mine dropped.

'You have to be careful with answers; they are never what you want them to be, don't you think?'

Then, with the tip of his left shoe, he flicked the piece of moss he had broken away with his cane into the water. Fresh and green, it waltzed round before gliding into the middle of the canal and sinking.

I turned back to Destinat. He had disappeared.

Life picked up again, as they say, and the war ended. The hospital gradually emptied, as did the streets. The cafés did less business, as did Agathe Blachart. Sons and husbands came home, some whole, others damaged. A good many never came back, of course. There was always the hope for some, though, despite the evidence, that they would come round the end of the street, walk into the house, sit down at the table and ask for a jug of wine. Those families whose men worked at the factory had come through the war almost untouched. Others, though, were emerging from four terrible years. The gulf between them deepened, especially when a dead loved one came to fester in it. Some people would no longer speak to each other, others began to hate.

Bassepin started up his trade with the memorials. One of the first ones he supplied was ours: a soldier with the flag in his left hand, rifle in his right, his body straining forwards, with one knee bent and next to him the Gallic cockerel, a huge proud creature raised on his spurs and just about to crow.

The mayor inaugurated our memorial on 11 November 1920. He gave a speech – all quivering pride and rolling eyes – then read out the names of the forty-three lads from our little town who had fallen, leaving a pause after each name so that Aimé Lachepot, the rural policeman, could deliver an earnest drum roll. Weeping women in black held on to little children who strained over to Margot Gagneure's shop with its window full of liquorice and honey-flavoured lollipops.

Then the standard was raised. The brass band played a gloomy tune and everyone stood to attention, staring straight ahead. As soon as we could we all hurried over to the *mairie* where a little reception had been laid on. The dead were forgotten in sparkling wine and bread and pâté. People chatted, even laughed. It lasted an hour and everyone promised to put on this little show of heavy hearts and memories every year.

Destinat was at the ceremony, in the front row. I was two metres behind him. He did not come to the *mairie*, but slowly made his way back to the château alone.

Even though he had been retired four years, Destinat still went to V occasionally. Old Gloomy would have the horses harnessed for ten to ten. On the stroke of ten, Destinat would sit himself in the carriage and they'd set off, and there was no sparing the horses. Once in town, he would walk through the streets, always the same route: Rue Marville, Place de la Préfecture, Allée Baptiste-Villemaux, Rue Plassis, Rue d'Autun, Square Fidon and the Rue des Bourelles. Old Gloomy followed in the carriage, twenty metres behind, trying to steady the horses which jogged and crapped impatiently. When Destinat came across people who knew him he tilted his head but never replied to their greeting.

At noon he would go into Le Rébillon, where he was welcomed by Bourrache. He still had his table, ate the same food and drank the same wine as in the days when he could call for heads. The only difference was that now he stayed on after coffee. The room emptied but Destinat stayed. Bourrache would come over to join him with a bottle of the best brandy, and two little glasses, and sit down across from Destinat. Bourrache would swill down his glass, but Destinat sniffed it only, never brought it to his lips.

Then they would talk.

'Talk about what?' I asked Bourrache once, much later.

It was as if he was looking at something very far away, at a picture that was out of focus. His eyes started to shine.

'About my little one,' he said, and great tears rolled down his rough cheeks.

'He did the talking, I just listened really. You'd have thought he knew her better than me, and yet when she was still with us I never saw him speak to her, never a word when she brought him his bread or a jug of water. It was as if he knew everything about her. He used to paint a picture of her for me, he told me about her, her complexion, her hair, her little birdy voice, the shape of her mouth, the colour of her lips too. He talked about painters I'd never heard of, told me she could have been in one of their paintings. And he asked every sort of question: what she was like, her little habits, the little things she said, the illnesses she'd had, about when she was a baby. I had to tell him about her, on and on, he never tired of it.

'And every time, it was the same: "Would you like to talk about her, my dear Bourrache?" he would say. And I didn't really want to, it made my heart hurt all the rest of the day and into the evening, but I didn't dare say that, so I talked. An hour, two, I think we could have talked for days and he wouldn't have minded. I found it strange, this passion he had for my dead little one, but I thought it must be because he was getting old, maybe he was going a bit senile, that was all, and the fact that he was on his own and hadn't had any children must have been preying on his mind.

'One day he asked me if I had a photograph of her that I could give him. Well, I mean, photographs, they're expensive, I only had three, and one of them was of my three girls. It was Belle's godmother who'd had it done, and paid for it. She took them to Isidore Kopierck, you know, the Russian on the Rue des Etats. He got them to pose, the older two sitting on the ground, all grass and flowers behind them, and Belle in the middle, standing, and smiling. So lovely, like the Blessed Virgin herself. I had three copies of that photograph, one for each of the girls. I gave Belle's one to him. You'd have thought I'd given him a gold mine! He started to shake all over, couldn't stop thanking me, and shaking my hand so hard I thought he'd pull it off.

'The last time he came was the week before he died. Still the same story, the meal, the coffee, the brandy, the talking. The questions, the same ones, then he said, almost in a whisper, like he was pronouncing a verdict: "She never knew evil. She was gone before she could know it. But the rest of us, it's made us so ugly . . ." then he stood up, and shook my hand very slowly. I helped him into his coat, gave him his hat, and he looked all round the room, as if he was measuring it up. I opened the door and said, "Until next time, Monsieur le Procureur." He smiled but he didn't say anything. He left.'

I have come to realise in these months how painful it is to write. It hurts your hand, and your heart. Man was not made for it. And what good is it anyway? What good is it? Even if Belle de jour had died, with all the mystery surrounding that, even with the death of the Breton boy still darkening a corner of my conscience, even with all that, had Clémence been with me, I would not have scribbled these pages. Just having her here would have been enough. It would have distanced me from the past and given me strength. Deep down, it is for her, and her alone, that I write, to try to fool myself that she is waiting for me, somewhere, wherever. And that she can hear everything I say.

Writing means I can live for two.

When you are on your own for a long time you talk out loud, to the walls themselves sometimes. What I am doing is not so different. I often wonder how the Prosecutor chose to spend his time. To whom did he dedicate his thoughts? Who did he talk to, in his mind? One widower understands another. In fact, there were plenty of things which could have brought us together.

xxii

On 27 September 1921, as I was crossing the Rue des Pressoirs, I failed to see a motor car coming and was knocked down. I remember, at the moment my head struck the edge of the pavement, thinking of Clémence, as if she was alive and would have to be told that her husband had had an accident. I remember, in that fraction of a second, I was annoyed with myself for not looking, for having my head in the clouds, for causing her anxiety. Then I passed out. It felt quite soothing, I was almost happy. When I came to at the hospital, they told me that I had been in that strange sleep for seven whole days. Seven days out of my life, seven days of which I have no recollection. There was only blackness, a mellow darkness. The doctors thought I would never wake. They were wrong. I was unlucky.

'You were at death's door!' one of them told me, delighted I was awake. He was a young lad with beautiful darting brown eyes, and all his youthful illusions still intact. I did not reply. In all of that darkness I had not found the woman I loved, and still love. I did not hear her or feel her. The doctor must have been wrong: I must have been very far from death, because she was not there.

They kept me in for two more weeks. I was strangely weak. I did not know any of the nurses, though they seemed to know me. They brought me soup, herbal tea and stew. I asked after

Madame de Flers and they smiled at me, but did not answer. They must have thought I was delirious.

When it was decided that I could talk without tiring myself too much, the mayor came to see me. He shook my hand. Told me I had come very close. That he had been in quite a state. Then he rummaged through his deep pockets and took out a bag of sweets which he had gone and bought specially. The sweets were all stuck together. He put the bag down on the bedside table, slightly apologetically.

'I wanted to bring you a really good bottle, but, well, it's not allowed in here, so I thought . . . Mind you, these ones, the woman at the patisserie fills them with cherry brandy!'

He laughed and I laughed to make him happy. I wanted to talk, to ask him questions, but he put his finger to his lips, as if to say we had plenty of time. The nurses had told him to handle me carefully, not to talk too much and not to let me talk too much. We stayed there like that for a few moments, looking at each other, looking at the sweets, at the ceiling, and at the window through which you could see nothing but a corner of sky, no trees, no hills, no clouds.

Then he stood up, shook my hand for a long time, and left. He did not tell me that Destinat had died. I learned that two days later from Father Lurant. It had happened the day after my accident. He died in the simplest way possible. No fuss, no pain, on a beautiful red and gold autumn day, still tinged with the memory of summer, hardly a hint of chill in the air.

He had gone out in the middle of the afternoon for his walk in the grounds as usual, and he had sat down, as usual, on the bench overlooking the Guerlante, hands resting on his cane. He usually stayed there for just under an hour before going back in.

On that day, because she had not seen him come back, Barbe went out and saw him in the distance, still on the bench.

She did not see his face, only his back. Reassured, she went back into the kitchen to prepare the roast. But once the joint of veal was ready and the vegetables were all peeled, chopped and popped into the pot, she realised that she still had not heard him come in. She went back out, and saw him still on his bench, oblivious to the mist rising up from the river and the darkness that was enveloping the trees in the park as the squabbling crows gathered. Barbe decided to go over and let her master know that supper was ready. She went across the gardens, drew near and called him, but got no reply. When she was close, only a few metres away, she had a feeling of foreboding. She walked slowly round the bench and saw Destinat, still quite straight, eyes wide open, two hands clasped on the knob of his cane, as dead as dead can be.

People often say that life is unfair, but death is even more so, the dying part at least. Some suffer and others slip away like a sigh. There may be no justice in this world, but there is none in the leaving of it, either. Destinat had gone without a sound, without warning either. Quite alone, as he had lived.

Father Lurant told me that he had had an official funeral attended by everyone deemed important and beautiful. The men were in black morning suits, the women's faces obscured by grey veils. The bishop had made the journey, the *préfet*, and an Under-Secretary of State. The entire cortège went on to the cemetery, where Destinat's successor gave the address. Then Ostrane did his bit, just as he should, with his enthusiasm and his shovel.

When I came out of hospital, the first thing I did before going home was go to the cemetery to see Clémence, and Destinat. I walked very slowly, with the stiffness in my left leg I have not lost to this day. It makes me look like a veteran, me who was never in a war!

I sat down by Clémence's grave and told her about my

accident, my fear that she would be worried about me, my long soothing sleep and the disappointed awakening. I cleaned the marble, pulled out the weeds growing along the bottom of the stone, and used my palm to rub off the lichen which was growing over the cross. Then I blew her a kiss.

Destinat's tomb was almost invisible under the bejewelled wreaths, and ribbons, cards and messages of condolence, some still unopened. The bouquets had completely spoiled and shed their rusted petals on the surrounding gravel. He was there, I thought, with his wife at last. He had taken his time. A whole lifetime. I thought about the distinguished figure he had been, his silence, his mystery, that mixture of seriousness and distance he carried about him, and I wondered whether I stood by the tomb of a murderer or an innocent man.

xxiii

A few years later, after Barbe's funeral, I told myself that it was high time I visited the château. The key she had entrusted to me made me the lord of an orphaned estate. I walked from the graveyard to that huge house as if something was waiting for me there, and at last I dared to meet it.

As I turned the key in the tall door I felt I was breaking the seal on some mysterious envelope. And the envelope was full of sheets of paper on which the truth had always been inscribed in delicate ink. And I do not mean simply the truth about the *Affaire*, I mean my own truth, the truth about what made me a man, a man getting on with his life.

While the Prosecutor was alive I had never set foot inside the château. Not me. A rag amongst silk handkerchiefs, that's what I would have been there. I had brushed past it, circled round it, seen it from afar in its constant blaze of glory, lofty roofs of slate and copper gables. And then there had been Lilia Verhareine's death, and Destinat waiting for me at the top of the steps, on the porch, devastated, and the two of us walking like condemned men towards the little house, going up to the bedroom . . .

The château was not the home of someone who had died: it had been emptied of life long before that. The fact that the Prosecutor had lived there, and Barbe and Old Gloomy too, did not change this. As you stepped into the hall, you could feel it. This house had died, stopped breathing years ago, stopped echoing to the sound of footsteps, voices, laughter, whispers, arguments, dreams and sighs.

It was not cold inside. There was no dust, no cobwebs, none of the mess you expect when you force the lock of a tomb. The hall, still with its black-and-white chequered floor, lay like a huge draughts board from which the draughts had been stolen. There were vases, occasional tables, Dresden couples dancing on gilded consoles, their minuets interrupted by centuries. A large mirror presented the visitor with his own face, and I saw that I had become fatter, older and uglier than I had imagined, a distorted version of my own father, a grotesque resurrection.

In one corner a large china dog kept guard with its jaws open, its canines in dazzling enamel and its tongue thick and red. From the ceiling, which was so high you had to strain to see it, hung a chandelier, at least three tonnes in weight, adding to the unease of whoever stood below it. On the wall opposite the door there was a long painting, all creams, silvers and blues, of a very young woman in a ball-gown, with a diadem of pearls on her forehead. The years had darkened the varnish but I could still see that she was pale, her mouth barely pink, her eyes terribly melancholy. She seemed to be making an effort to smile, held herself elegantly erect and yet looked somehow poignantly abandoned. As one hand worked to open a fan of lace and mother of pearl, the other rested on the head of a stone lion.

I stayed a long time looking at this woman whom I had never seen, and never known: Clélia de Vincey – Clélia Destinat. The mistress of the house, silently surveying her clumping visitor. I very nearly turned on my heel and fled. What right had I to come here, stirring up the old ghosts in that stagnant air?

But the face did not seem hostile, just surprised, and at the same time kindly. I spoke to her – I no longer really remember what I said, it hardly matters. She belonged to another age: clothes, hair, expression, pose, all made her seem like a sumptuous, fragile exhibit in a forgotten museum. Her face reminded me of other faces. Faces moving, dancing, changing, growing young, growing old again. I could not pick any single one out, could not look at it properly, or recognise it.

I could not have lived with a painting of Clémence under my eyes like that, every day, every hour. I destroyed the pictures I had of her, down to the last one, down to the smallest, threw them all into the fire one day. Those lying, smiling photographs. Seeing them would have increased my pain, like loading up an already laden carriage at the risk of sending the whole thing toppling into the ditch. I don't know how Destinat had lived with this one.

Perhaps in the end he stopped seeing it, perhaps it had become just a painting, not a portrait of the woman he had loved and lost? Perhaps he had reached that museum-like state of disembodiment which spares us when we look at varnished faces, convinces us that they never lived as we live, never breathed, slept, never suffered?

The half-closed shutters gave the rooms a pleasant shadowiness. Everything was well-ordered, as if the owner was expected back from his travels at any moment. The strangest thing was there was no smell. A house that doesn't smell is a dead house.

I stayed there for a long time, on that peculiar journey, an unhindered intruder. Nevertheless, I trod a clearly marked route even if I didn't know it. The château was like a shell and I followed its spiral round, heading slowly towards its centre, passing mundane rooms – kitchen, storerooms, laundry room, linen room, salon, dining room, smoking room – until I arrived at the library.

It was not very large, but its walls were completely covered with beautiful books. There was a desk and on it a writing set, a lamp, a simple paperknife and a black leather blotter. Two deep armchairs stood on either side of the desk. One of them was as good as new. The other held the imprint of a body, the leather cracked and shinier in some places than others. I sat down in the newer one. It felt comfortable. The chairs faced each other: opposite me, then, was the one in which Destinat had spent so many hours, reading or thinking about nothing.

All those books on the walls, like soldiers in a paper army, absorbed every sound. You could hear nothing of the world outside, no wind, no rumble from the factory even though it was nearby, no birdsong. There was a book open on Destinat's chair, upside down on the armrest. It was a very old book with dog-eared pages that had probably been fingered for a lifetime. Pascal's *Pensées*. I have it beside me now. It lies open at the very page it did then. And on that page, amid the sanctimonious ideas and muddled words, shining like a pair of gold earrings on a dungheap, are two sentences, two sentences underlined in pencil by Destinat's hand. I know them by heart:

> *'The last act is a bloody one however beautiful the rest of the performance may have been. Earth is finally thrown down upon the head, and that is it for ever.'*

Some words can send a shiver down your spine, take all the strength from your arms and legs. Those ones, for example. I know nothing of Pascal's life, and I hardly care, but I am pretty sure that he thought precious little of this performance he is talking about. Like me. Like Destinat, probably. He too must have tasted the sourness, and lost the faces he loved too soon. Otherwise he would never have been able to say that. When you live amongst flowers, you do not think about mud.

Book in hand, I went from room to room. And there were

plenty of them. All the same when it came down to it. Bare rooms. By which I mean that they had always been bare, neglected, with no memories, no past, no echoes. They had all the sad pointlessness of a tool that has never been used. They had never experienced the bustle of human activity, the odd scratch or two, the breath against their windows, heavy bodies in canopied beds, children's games, anger behind closed doors, tears disappearing between floorboards.

Destinat's bedroom was at the far end of a corridor, slightly apart from the others. Withdrawn. Its door was painted a dark colour close to garnet. I knew straight away that it was his room. Where else would it have been but there at the end of that corridor, like some formal passageway which forced you to go down it in a particular way, solemnly and cautiously. Engravings hung on the walls, long-forgotten faces, the decayed leftovers of other centuries, bewigged, ruffed, moustachioed, Latin inscriptions like necklaces around their throats. Portraits of the dead. I felt as if they were all watching me as I walked towards that large red door. I called them every name I could think of, just to give myself courage.

Destinat's room was nothing like the others. The bed was narrow, a monk's bed: iron bedposts and a simple mattress, no trimmings, no tester hanging from the ceiling. The walls were simply lined with grey, no paintings or decorations. Beside the bed stood a small table with a crucifix on it. At the foot of the bed there was a washstand with jug and basin. A high-backed chair. A little desk with nothing on it. No book, no paper, no pen.

The room was like the man himself. Cold, silent, it made you uncomfortable but it inspired respect. It had drawn a sense of distance from the man who slept there, impervious to laughter for ever. The very orderliness of the place endorsed the idea of dead hearts.

I had the Pascal book in my hand and went over to the window from which there was a lovely view of the Guerlante, the little canal, and the bench on which death had found Destinat, and the little house in which Lilia Verhareine had lived.

I had come as close as I could to what his life had been. I do not mean his life as a public prosecutor, but his internal life, his true life, the life we hide under pomade, courtesy, work and conversation. His whole universe could be summed up by this empty room, these cold walls, these few pieces of furniture. It was almost as if I was inside his mind. I would not have been surprised to see him, to hear him say that he had been expecting me and that I had taken my time. That room was so far removed from life that, had a dead man appeared there, it would not have shocked me so very much. But the dead have other things to do.

In the drawers of the desk there were neat rows of block calendars, with all their pages torn off so only the stumps were left showing the year. Dozens of them, witnesses to thousands of days gone, destroyed, thrown away like the thin pages. Destinat had kept them all. To each his own rosary.

The largest drawer was locked. I remembered the little key on the end of the chain, next to the watch, and I knew there was little point looking for it because I knew it was inside a tomb. What would have been left of it, or of the pocket in which it lay, now all rust and rags?

I forced the drawer with my knife. The wood gave way with a little spray of splinters.

There was only one thing inside. I recognised it straight away and stopped breathing. Nothing seemed real any more. It was a small notebook, a narrow rectangular one covered in pretty red morocco leather. The last time I had seen it, it had been in Lilia Verhareine's hands. How many years ago? That was the day I had climbed to the crest of the hill, and caught her looking out over the great field of the dead. It was suddenly as if she had come into the room, laughing, and had stopped abruptly, amazed to see me there.

I picked the notebook up very quickly, afraid it would burn me, and fled like a thief.

I am not really sure what Clémence would have thought of it all, but I felt ashamed. The notebook weighed heavily in my pocket.

I ran, and I kept running. I had to knock back half a bottle of brandy at home before I got my breath back, or recovered any sense of calm.

I waited until evening, the notebook on my knees, not daring to open it, sitting there looking at it like that for hours, as if it were a living thing, secret and alive. By evening my head was burning. I had no feeling in my legs any more, I'd held them clamped together so hard. I could only feel the notebook. It was a heart, a heart – I was quite sure – which would start beating as soon as I touched the cover and opened it. A heart into which I was about to break, like a burglar.

13th December 1914
My love,

At last I am close to you. Today I arrived in P, a little town just a few kilometres from the front where you are. I was given the most charming welcome here. The mayor came rushing over as if I were the Messiah. The school is neglected. I shall take the place of the schoolmaster, who was seriously ill, they tell me. His lodgings were in such a deplorable state they'll have to find me somewhere else to live. For now, I shall sleep at the hotel. The mayor brought me here. He's a great thickset peasant trying to play the part of a young man. You would probably find him funny. I miss you so much. But knowing you're near me, knowing we're breathing the same air, seeing the same clouds, the same sky – all that is comforting. Take care of yourself, be very careful. I love you and send you my tender kisses.

Your Lily

16th December 1914
My love,

I have moved into a wonderful place, a dolls' house in the grounds of a beautiful house. The locals call it the château. They are exaggerating a little, it is not really a château, but a charming spot all the same. It was the mayor's idea. We went to see the owner together. He is an elderly gentleman, a widower who is the public prosecutor in V. The mayor outlined the request to him while I waited outside the house. Then I was called in. The Prosecutor didn't speak a single word to me. I smiled and said hello. He stayed there with my hand in his, for a very long time, as if surprised to see me. An infinite sadness emanates from every inch of him. In the end he gave the mayor his consent, bade me goodbye and we left.

The little house hasn't been lived in for a long time. I need to organise it. I'd like you to see it some day. I miss you so much. You can write to me in my name, at this address, the Château, rue des Champs-Fleury, P. I can't wait to hear from you. Your last letter is now three weeks old. I hope you're not suffering too much, despite the cold. We can hear the artillery fire here day and night. It makes me shudder from head to toe. I'm frightened. I love you and send you my tender kisses.

Your Lily

23rd December 1914
My love,

I'm so worried. Still no news from you, and the artillery fire goes on and on. And yet they said this war wouldn't last long. If you only knew how I long to feel your arms around me, to huddle in your arms, to see your smile, your eyes. I want to be your wife. I want the war to end quickly so that I can marry you, and give you beautiful children to tug at your moustache! Oh, if your parents and mine hadn't been so stupid last year, we would already belong to each other, for life . . . If you ever write to them, don't tell them where I am. I left without telling them. They no longer exist as far as I'm concerned.

I'm taking my new work to heart here. The children are biddable. I like them and I think they like me. They bring me *little presents, an egg, a walnut, a piece of bacon. I feel at peace with them, and I forget my loneliness a little.*

Sorrow (that's the nickname I've given to my host, the Prosecutor) is waiting for me every day when I come home. He is out walking in his grounds and he greets me. He's a cold, lonely old man. His wife died when they were very young.

Christmas soon . . . remember our last Christmas, when we were so happy! Write to me soon, my love, write to me . . .

I love you and send you my tender kisses.

Your Lily

7th January 1915
My love,

A letter at last! It arrived this morning but you wrote it on the 26th of December. And to think we are so close to each other. Sorrow gave it to me himself. He must have guessed what sort of letter it was, but he didn't ask me any questions. He knocked on the door, bade me good day, gave me the envelope and left.

I cried with joy as I read your words. I have your letter close to my heart, yes close to my heart, right next to my skin, and it feels as if it's you who's there, the warmth of you, the smell of you, I close my eyes . . .

I'm so afraid for you. There is a clinic here and so many wounded men keep arriving. They come every day, whole lorry loads of them. I'm so frightened of seeing you amongst them. The poor things are in such a state, scarcely human, some don't even have faces any more, others moan as if they've lost their minds.

Look after yourself, my love. Think of me. I love you and want to be your wife. I send you my tender kisses.

Your Lily

23rd January 1915
My love,

I miss you. How many months already without seeing you, without talking to you, without touching you . . . Why is it you can't get any leave? I'm so sad. I try to put on a brave face for the children, but I feel the tears welling up inside me, and I turn to the blackboard so that they don't have any suspicions, and I write out words.

And yet I don't have anything to complain about. Everyone here is kind to me, and I'm happy in this little house. Sorrow still keeps his respectful distance from me, but never fails to greet me, by accident, at least once a day. Yesterday, I don't know whether it was because of the cold, but I think he went quite red. He has an old servant, Barbe. I get on well with her. Sometimes I eat with her and her husband.

I've taken to going up to the top of the hill every Sunday. There is a large meadow up there and you can see the whole horizon. You are there, my love. There are puffs of smoke, horrible explosions. I stay as long as I can, until I can no longer feel my feet or my hands because the cold is so raw, but I want to have some small share in your suffering. My poor love . . . How much longer will this go on?

I send you my tender kisses. I'm waiting for your letters.
Your Lily who loves you.

There were endless pages like that, covered in fine sloping handwriting like a delicate frieze. Endless pages reproducing endless letters sent by Lilia Verhareine to the man she loved, the man whom she had followed here.

His name was Bastien Francoeur, and he was twenty-four years old and a corporal in the 27th Infantry. She wrote to him every day, told him about the hours that seemed to drag, the way the children laughed, how Destinat blushed, the presents from Martial Maire (the village idiot who thought she was some sort of goddess), and the spring which had scattered snowdrops and crocuses in the park. She told him about all of this, in her slight hand, and equally slight sentences, behind which anyone who had known her could see her smile. She told him mostly about her love and her loneliness, all of which she hid from us, we who saw her every day and never suspected a thing.

The notebook did not contain her lover's letters. Anyway, she received very few: nine in eight months. She counted them, of course. She kept them and read them again and again. Where were they? Close to her heart perhaps, right next to her skin, as she said in one letter.

Why did he write so few letters back? Lack of time? Lack of a place to write? Lack of wanting? We always know what others are to us, but we never know what we are to them. Did he love her as much as she loved him? I would like to believe he did, but deep down I cannot be sure ot it.

Nevertheless, the little schoolmistress lived in these letters, her blood flowed into her words, and the lights in the little house must have burned late into the night. After she had finished correcting her pupils' work, she must have picked up her pen and written her letter, copying it out again into the red notebook. They had all been copied out, as if she was keeping a journal of absence, a calendar of orphaned days spent far from the man for whom she had exiled herself, a little like the pages Destinat tore from his calendars.

The name Sorrow appeared often. I think she grew fond of the solitary man who provided her accommodation. She spoke of him with tender irony, noticing, but not duped by, his efforts to please her, making fun of him (not unkindly) for blushing or stammering, for his outfits, and for the walks that took him round the little house, his eyes glancing up at her bedroom window. She found him amusing. And I swear that Lilia Verhareine was the one and only person who ever thought him funny.

That famous meal which Barbe had told me about appeared in a long letter, dated 15th April 1915:

My love,

Yesterday evening I was invited to dinner by Sorrow. For the first time. Everything was done by the book: I found a little invitation under my door three days ago – 'Monsieur le Procureur Pierre-Ange Destinat requests the pleasure of your company at dinner on 14th April at 8 o'clock.' *I got all ready for a meal in company, and it was just the two of us, him and me alone together in a vast dining room which could have held sixty people! À deux, like lovers! I'm teasing you! Sorrow, as I've already told you, is almost an old man. But yesterday he was like a government minister, or a chancellor, sitting in a tail coat smart enough for a night at the opera! The table was dazzling, the china, the table cloth, the silverware, I felt as if – I don't know, as if I were at Versailles, perhaps!*

It wasn't Barbe who waited on us, but a very young girl. How old can she have been? Eight, nine perhaps. She took her role very seriously, and seemed used to playing it. She sometimes poked the tip of her tongue out between her lips, as children do when they're concentrating. Sometimes I would catch her eye and she would smile at me. It was all a bit strange, being alone together, the meal, the little girl. Barbe told me today that the child is the daughter of an innkeeper in V and that she's called Belle, which suits her beautifully. Her father had made the meal, and everything was superb, even if we hardly touched a thing. I don't think I've ever seen such a feast, but I'm suddenly feeling ashamed talking to you about this when you must be eating so badly, and perhaps not even enough! Forgive me, my love, I'm so stupid . . . I try to amuse you and all I do is rub salt in your wounds . . . I miss you so much. Why don't you write to me more? Your last letter was more than ten weeks ago . . . And still no leave . . . I know that nothing has happened to you, I feel it, I feel it. Write to me, my love. Your words help me live, just as being close to you helps me live, even though I can't see you, even though I can't hold you. Sorrow was not very talkative during our dinner. He was as shy as a youth and sometimes, if I looked at him for any length of time, he would blush. When I asked him whether his solitude was a burden he seemed to think about it for a long time then he said in a deep, gentle voice: 'Being alone is the human condition, whatever happens.' I thought that was really beautiful, and also very untrue: you are not beside me, but it's as if I can feel you every moment, and I often speak to you, out loud. A little before midnight, he walked me to the door, and kissed my hand. I found it very romantic, and rather fusty too!

Oh my love, how much longer will this war go on? Sometimes, at night, I dream that you're beside me, I can feel you, I touch you in my sleep. And in the morning I don't open my eyes straight away, but stay in the dream a little longer, believing that it is real life, and that what's waiting for me in the day is the nightmare.

I'm dying because I'm not in your arms.

I send you a kiss as powerful as my love.

Your Lily

As time went by, bitterness began to creep into the young schoolteacher's letters, despondency, even hatred. This girl we had always seen with her luminous smile and kind words, her heart was slowly filling with venom and pain. She described how she was disgusted by the men she saw in town, all those who went off to the factory, clean and neat and fresh. Even the wounded loitering in the streets came in for a share of her angry resentment. She called them the Lucky Ones. But the person who actually carried off the prize, the one who got a faceful of it, was yours truly. When I read the letter that mentioned me I got quite a shock. It was written on the evening of that wretched day when I saw her on the crest of the hill, looking out over the plain as if she would find some meaning there.

4th June 1915

My love,

Your letters are like blotting paper now, I fold and unfold them, and read and re-read them so often, then I cry over them . . . This hurts, do you realise? I feel as if time is a monster born to keep apart those who love each other, to make them suffer. They're so lucky, these women I see every day, separated from their husbands for just a few hours a day, those children in the school who still have their fathers close by.

Today, I climbed up the hill as I do every Sunday, and came close to you. As I walked along the path I saw nothing but you, breathed only the smell of you, which I still remember. There was a strong wind up there carrying the sound of artillery fire. Banging, banging, banging . . . I cried to think of you under that deluge of iron and fire whose sinister flashes and smoke I could see. My love, where were you? Where are you? I stayed there for a long time, as usual. I couldn't take my eyes off that vast field of suffering in which you've been living for months.

I suddenly felt someone was behind me. It was a man, I know him by sight, he's an investigating officer, and I've always wondered what he could possibly have to do in this little town. He's older than you but still a young man. He's on the right side, with the cowards. He was looking at me stupidly, as if he'd stumbled across something forbidden. He had a shotgun in his hand, not one like yours for killing men or being killed, but for shooting game, I think, a ridiculous gun like a theatre prop or a child's toy. He stood there like a clown. At that moment I hated him more than anyone else in the world. He stammered a few words that I couldn't make out. I turned my back on him.

I would give the lives of thousands of men like him for a few seconds in your arms. I would cut the heads off them myself, just to feel your kisses on my lips again, to feel your hands and look into your eyes. It doesn't matter to me if I'm hateful. I couldn't care less about other people's opinions and morals. I would kill to have you alive. I hate death because it's indiscriminate.

Write to me, my love, write to me.

Every day without you is bitter suffering . . .
Your Lily

I did not resent her for it. It was justified. I really had been the idiot she described, and I probably still was. And I too would have killed to have Clémence back. I too thought the living were loathsome. I would wager that the Prosecutor felt the same. I would wager that life felt like a spit in the face to him.

I made my way through the notebook as if following a road through a blossoming countryside into a barbaric expanse of pus, acid and blood, black bile and burning marshes. Each day that passed changed Lilia Verhareine, even if we noticed nothing. The beautiful, delicate, gentle young woman was changing into a creature that roared in silence and ripped at itself inside. She was falling. And she could not stop.

In some letters it was her fiancé that she berated, reproaching him for the rarity of his replies, doubting his love. But the very next day she would festoon him with apologies and throw herself at his feet. Not that it made him write any more frequently.

I shall never know which camp he was in, this Bastien Francoeur. I shall never know what sort of light shone in his eyes when he opened one of Lilia's letters. I shall never know whether he kept them about him, like paper armour, and when they were about to make an assault, and all his life suddenly spun through his head like a grimacing carousel, did he read them through wearily, or did he laugh and scrumple them up and throw them into a muddy puddle?

The last letter, the last page of the notebook, was dated 3rd August 1915. It was a short letter in which she talked of her love, in simple words, and of the summer, about the huge days which were so beautiful but empty for someone alone and waiting. I am transcribing. Abbreviating a little, but not too much. I could copy it out, but I don't want to. It is already enough that Destinat and myself have laid eyes on the notebook, as if we had seen her naked body. There is no point in other people seeing these letters, particularly the last, which is sort of sacred, a farewell to the world, the last words, even if when she wrote them she could not have known they would be the last.

After that letter there is nothing else, just a blank page, pages and pages left blank. As blank as death itself.

Death in words.

When I say there is nothing else I am lying. I am doubly lying.

First of all there is a letter. But not from Lilia. A little sheet of paper slipped into the notebook, after her last words. It was written by one Captain Brandieu and is dated 27th July 1915, and it must have arrived at the Château on 4th August. I am sure that it must have.

This is what the Captain says:

Mademoiselle Verhareine,

I am writing to give you very sad news: ten days ago, during an assault on enemy lines, Corporal Bastien Francoeur was struck in the head by machine-gun fire. Helped by his men, he was brought back to our trench where a nurse could do nothing but confirm how very serious his wounds were. Unfortunately, Corporal Francoeur died a few minutes later, without regaining consciousness.

I can assure you that he died a soldier. He has been under my command for months now, and he has always behaved courageously, volunteering for the most dangerous missions. He was liked by his men and appreciated by his superiors.

I do not know the nature of your relationship with Corporal Francoeur, but as a number of letters from you have arrived since his death, it seemed right that I should inform you, as well as his family, of his tragic end.

Please believe, Mademoiselle Verhareine, that I understand your pain, and I hope you will accept my sincerest condolences.
Captain Charles-Louis Brandieu

It is strange how death takes you. Forget the knife, the bullet or the shell: a letter can be enough, a simple letter full of fine sentiments and kindness kills just as surely as a knife or a bullet.

Lilia Verhareine received that letter. She read it. I do not know whether she cried, wailed or kept quiet. I don't know. All I know is that a few hours later we were in her bedroom, the Prosecutor and I, and she was dead. We looked at each other and we did not understand. At least, I did not understand. He may have already known: he had already taken the little red notebook.

Why had he taken it? To continue their conversation, to keep her smiles and her words with him? Probably.

So he was dead, the soldier, the lover, the man for whom she had left everything, for whom she had climbed to the top of the hill every Sunday, for whom she picked up her pen every day, for whom her heart beat. What about him, what did he see when death battered in his skull? Lilia? Some other girl? Nothing? A mystery and a trifle.

I have often pictured Destinat reading and re-reading that notebook, entering into this testament of love. It must have hurt him, seeing himself called Sorrow, being made fun of, but in such a gentle, tender way – at least he did not get it full in the face as I did.

Reading and re-reading, endlessly, like turning an hourglass over and over, spending your time watching the sand sifting through, and nothing else.

I said earlier that I was doubly lying: there was not just

that letter slipped inside the notebook. There were also three photographs. Three, stuck one beside the other, on the last page, like a film had been frozen. It was Destinat who had put them there.

In the first I recognised the girl who had been the model for the large portrait in the hall of the château: Clélia de Vincey. She must have been about seventeen at the time. She stood in a field of long grass dotted with fragrant meadow-sweet: a pretty flower we call Queen of the Meadow round here. Laughing. In country clothes, her utter elegance heightened by their simplicity. A wide-brimmed hat threw a shadow over her face, but her eyes caught the light, and there was her smile, the bright sunlight on her hand holding the brim of her hat as it was lifted by the wind. All this gave her face a dazzling loveliness. She was the true queen of the meadow.

The second photograph had been snipped from a larger one (I could tell by the smooth edges and by the shape). In it a happy little girl looked straight ahead. Destinat's scissors had isolated Belle de jour from the photograph of the three girls that Bourrache had given him. 'Like the Blessed Virgin', her father had said. And he was right. The child's face had a religious quality, a beauty without artifice, a simple splendour.

In the third photograph, Lilia Verhareine was leaning against a tree, her hands flat against the bark, her chin tilted upwards, her mouth half open, as if waiting to be kissed by whoever was taking the photograph. Just as we had known her. Only she had never smiled at us like that, never. It was a smile full of desire, full of passion, there was no mistaking it, and seeing her like that was very disturbing, as if she had been suddenly unmasked and you could see who she really was, and what she was capable of doing for the man she loved, or to herself.

Still, the most peculiar thing about it all – and it was not the odd drop I had had that made me see it – was the feeling that I was looking at three portraits of the same face, taken at different ages, and in different periods.

Belle de jour, Clélia and Lilia were like three incarnations of the same soul. A soul which endowed the bodies it assumed with the same smile, the same gentleness and fire. The same beauty, visited and revisited, born and destroyed, appearing and gone. Seeing them like that side by side made your head spin. You could go from one to the other but it was still the same one. There was something pure and yet diabolical about it all, a mixture of serenity and terror. You could almost believe that beauty lives on, whatever happens, despite the passage of time, and that whatever once was will return.

I thought of Clémence. I could have added a fourth photograph, completed the round. I was going mad. I closed the notebook. My head hurt. It was too much. And all because of three little photographs placed side by side by an old man well acquainted with boredom.

I nearly burned the lot.

But I did not. Professional habits die hard. You do not destroy evidence. Evidence of what? That we do not see people as they are until they are dead? Not one of us ever said: 'Oh look, Bourrache's little girl and Lilia Verhareine are as alike as two peas in a pod!' Barbe never said to me: 'The little teacher is just like the late Madame Destinat!'

Perhaps only death could reveal that. Perhaps the Prosecutor and I were the only ones who could see it. Perhaps we were alike. Alike as two madmen!

When I think of Destinat's long, well-tended fingers, those lined and sinewy hands, I see them late on a winter's afternoon, around Belle de jour's fragile neck, as the smile fades from the child's face and a huge question comes into her eyes. I imagine the scene only, that scene which did happen, which did not happen and I tell myself that Destinat was not strangling a child, but a memory, a suffering, that he suddenly had in his hands, under his fingers, the ghost of Clélia and the ghost of Lilia Verhareine, that he was trying to rid himself of her once and for all, so that he no longer had to see her, them, no longer had to hear them, no longer had to chase them hopelessly in his dreams, no longer had to love them in vain.

It's difficult to be done with the dead. To make them disappear. How many times have I tried! Everything would be so much easier if it were not so.

Other faces would have appeared in the face of that child, that child met by chance, at the very end of a snowy, icy day, as night began to fall, and with it all the painful shadows. Love and murder would suddenly have become confused, as if, in that moment, you could only kill what you loved.

I have lived a long time with the idea of Destinat as a man who killed in error, in hope, in memory, in terror. I found the idea beautiful. It took nothing away from the crime, in fact it made it into something dazzling, something less sordid. Killer and victim as martyrs. So rare.

Then one day a letter arrived. With letters we can tell when they are sent but we can't tell why they sometimes never arrive. Or why they take so long. Perhaps the little corporal wrote to Lilia Verhareine every day? Perhaps his letters are still circulating somewhere, getting lost in alleys and byways, waiting to arrive.

The letter I am now talking about was posted in Rennes on 23 March 1919. It took six years to arrive. Six years to cross France.

It was from a fellow officer, not someone I knew or who knew me. He must have sent the same letter to all the other

[177]

investigating officers like me dozing in little towns close to what had been the front.

What this Alfred Vignot wanted was to trace a lad he had not seen since 1916. We received requests like this from *mairies*, families, police forces, all the time. The war had caused great turmoil, shuffling hundreds of thousands of men about. Some were dead, others survived. Some had gone home, others had wanted to start their lives all over again, with no one any the wiser. That great butchery had not only carved up bodies and minds, it had made it possible for a few to be presumed dead so that they could go and test the water a long way away from home. It would take a very clever man to prove that they were actually alive especially when it was so easy to change your name and your papers. About a million and a half lads would never need their names and papers again. Quite a lot of choice! A lot of dirty bastards popped up again, all shiny and clean, far from the places which had known their filth.

Vignot's missing man had a death on his conscience, a girl he had tortured meticulously – the details were there in the letter – before strangling her and raping her. The crime had taken place in May 1916. And it took Vignot three years to conclude his enquiries, gather all the proof, be sure of the facts. The victim's name was Blanche Fen'vech. She was ten years old. She had been found at the bottom of a ditch, less than a kilometre from the village of Plouzagen, where she lived. She had gone, as she did every evening, to fetch four wretched cows from the meadow. I did not have to read it to guess who Vignot was looking for. The moment I opened the envelope, a sort of shiver passed through me.

The name of this killer was Le Floc, Yann Le Floc. He was nineteen years old at the time of the incident. My little Breton.

I did not reply to Vignot. Each to his own shit. He was

probably right about Le Floc, but that didn't change anything. The girls were dead, the one in Brittany and the one in our town. And the boy was dead too, shot according to the rules. And, deep down, I felt that Vignot might be wrong, that perhaps he had his own reasons for shouldering the case onto the boy, just as the worthless Mierck and Matziev had had theirs. How would anyone ever know?

Another strange thing – I had grown accustomed to living with mystery, with doubt, half-light, hesitation, a lack of answers and certitudes. Replying to Vignot would have made all that disappear: all of a sudden there would have been light. Destinat would have been wiped clean and the little Breton plunged into darkness. It was too simple. One of the two had killed, that was for sure, but either could have done it and when it came down to it, was there a difference between the intention and the crime?

I took Vignot's letter and lit my pipe with it, made smoke and ash of it. Keep looking, my man. I will not be the only one on the case! Perhaps that was my revenge. A way of proving to myself that I was not the only one scratching through the earth with my nails, trying to find the dead and to make them speak. We need to know that there are others like us.

xxvii

We are coming to the end of this story. The end of my own story. The tombs have been closed a long time, mouths have been shut, and the dead are merely names worn into tombstones: Belle, Lilia, Destinat, Old Gloomy, Barbe, Adélaïde Siffert, the Breton boy and the typesetter, Mierck, Gachentard, Bourrache's wife, Hippolyte Lucy, Mazerulles, Clémence . . . I often picture them, all of them, in the cold dark earth. I know that their eyes have been hollowed and empty for a long time now and that their clasped hands no longer have any flesh.

If anyone asks how I have filled the years leading to this point, today, I would not be able to answer them. I did not see time pass, even though it seemed to pass so slowly. I kept a flame burning, and I interrogated the darkness without gleaning more than snatches of answers.

The whole of my life depended on this dialogue with a few dead people. It kept me going, till the end. I have talked to Clémence. And to the others. There were very few days when I did not make them appear, slipping back into their familiar gestures and words, to ask me whether I had heard them properly.

When I thought I had at last got a glimmer of the truth, something else would come along to blow out the light and throw cinders in my eyes. I had to start everything all over again.

Perhaps that is what has made me endure, this dialogue with a voice, always the same voice, always my own voice; that and the opacity of this crime where the only guilty party may well be the opacity of our lives. Life certainly is strange. Do we ever find out why we come into the world, and why we stay in it? Delving into the *Affaire* as I have done was probably a way of avoiding the real question, the one we refuse to voice on our lips and in our minds, or in our souls which are indeed neither white nor black but grey, as Joséphine said.

As for me, I am here. I have not lived. I have survived. A shiver runs through me. I open a bottle of wine and I drink as I think about the time I've lost.

I think I've said everything. Said everything about what I thought I was. I have told you everything, or nearly. There is only one thing left to say, perhaps the most difficult, the thing I have never whispered even to Clémence. I'll drink some more, I need to courage to say it, to say it to you, Clémence, because it is for you alone that I have been talking and writing, from the beginning. It has always been for you.

The baby, our baby, I could not give him a name, or even really look at him. I never even kissed him as a father should have done.

A nun in a wimple, a great tall creature dry as an autumn fruit forgotten in the oven, brought him to me a week after you died. She said: 'This is your child. He's yours. And you'll have to bring him up.' Then she put the white bundle in my arms and went away. It was asleep, all warm and smelling of milk. So soft. His face peeped out of the linen like the infant Jesus in a crib. His eyes were closed, his cheeks round, so round that his mouth almost disappeared into them. I looked at him to find your features in his face, some memory of you, hoping you could have given me this beyond your death. But he didn't look like anything, certainly not you. He looked like a newborn baby, just arrived in the daylight after a long cosy night spent in a place that we all forget. An innocent, as they say. A man child. Our future. But not for me, for me he was none of that. For me, he was just your assassin, the little assassin with no conscience and no remorse, with whom I had to live now that you were no longer there. He had killed you to come to me, he had dug in his elbows and God knew what else to be alone, alone with me, and I would never see your face again or kiss your skin, while he would grow bigger every day, would break his teeth and go on devouring, would have hands to take things and eyes to see them, and then, later, words, words to speak his fat lies to whoever wanted to hear them: that he had never known you, that you died as he was born, when the real truth was that he killed you to be born.

I did not think about it for very long. It came all by itself. I took a big pillow and I made his face disappear. I waited, and waited. He did not move. To use the words of those who judge us down here, there was no premeditation: it was the only thing I could do and I did it. I took away the pillow and I cried. I cried and thought of you, not of him.

Then I went to fetch Hippolyte Lucy, the doctor, to tell him the child was not breathing. He went into the bedroom. The child was on the bed. He still had that face like an innocent, peaceful and monstrous.

The doctor undressed him. He brought his cheek close to the little closed mouth. He listened to the heart that was no longer beating. He said nothing. He closed his bag and turned to me and we looked at each other for a long time. He knew. I knew that he knew, but he said nothing. He left the room and left me alone with the little body.

I had him buried beside you. Ostrane told me that newborn babies disappeared into the ground like perfume on the wind, before you even had time to notice them. He told me that without meaning any harm. He seemed to marvel at it.

I did not put his name on the tombstone.

The worst thing is that, even today, I feel no remorse and I would do it all over again without any fuss, just as I did it without any fuss then. I am not proud of it. I am not ashamed of it either. It was not pain that made me do it. It was emptiness. The emptiness in which I have stayed, but in which I wanted to stay alone. He would have been an unhappy little creature living and growing beside me, and his life would have been an emptiness filled by one single question, a great dark bottomless pit round which I paced constantly, talking to you all the time so that my words formed a wall that I could try to cling to.

Yesterday I went and hung around the Bridge of Thieves. Do you remember? How old were we? Not quite twenty? You were wearing a dress the colour of redcurrants. My stomach felt tight. We were on the bridge and we were looking at the river. The current, you said, is our lives flowing by. Look how far it goes, look how beautiful it is, over there, between the water lilies and the long streaming weeds and the clay banks. I did not dare put my hand round your waist. I had such a tight knot in my stomach that I could hardly breathe. Your eyes were looking away into the distance. Mine were looking at the nape of your neck. I could smell your heliotrope perfume and the scent of the river, all fresh with crushed weeds. Then, when I least expected it, you turned towards me, smiled, and kissed me. It was the first time. The water flowed under the bridge. The world was bright as a beautiful Sunday. Time stood still.

Yesterday I stayed on the Bridge of Thieves for a long time. The river is the same. There are still the big water lilies, the long streaming weeds, the clay banks. Still the fresh smell of crushed weeds, but only that smell now.

A child came up to me. A boy with pale eyes. He said: 'Are

you looking at the fish?' Then he went on, slightly disappointed: 'There are masses of them, but you never see them.' I said nothing. There are so many things that we never see. He leant over next to me and we stayed like that for a good while, listening to the frogs and watching the eddies. He and I. The beginning and the end. After some time I left. The boy followed me for a while, then he disappeared.

Now it is all over. I have used up all my time and I am no longer afraid of the emptiness. You may be thinking that I too am a bastard, that I am no better than the others. You are right. Of course you are right. Forgive me for everything I have done, but forgive me especially for everything I have not done.

I hope that soon you will be able to judge me, face to face. I hope that God does exist, and has all his holy paraphernalia with him, all the nonsense they stuffed into us when we were little. You'll have trouble recognising me. You left a young man, you'll find almost an old man now, all worn and wounded. But you, I know you haven't changed. That is the thing about the dead.

I took down Gachentard's shotgun earlier on, took it apart, oiled it, cleaned it, put it together again and loaded it. I knew I would finish my story today. The shotgun is right next to me now. Outside, the day is clear and mild. It's Monday. It's morning. That's all. I have nothing left to say. I have said everything. Confessed everything. It's time.

I can join you now.